BENJAMIN SVETKEY

LEADING
MAN

As a writer and editor at *Entertainment Weekly,*
Benjamin Svetkey spent two decades flying around
the world visiting film sets and writing stories about
movie stars. He currently lives in Santa Monica,
California, with his wife, Lenka, and their three-
year-old daughter, Chloe.

LEADING
MAN

LEADING
MAN

BENJAMIN
SVETKEY

VINTAGE CONTEMPORARIES

VINTAGE BOOKS

A DIVISION OF RANDOM HOUSE, INC.

NEW YORK

A VINTAGE CONTEMPORARIES ORIGINAL, SEPTEMBER 2013

Library of Congress Cataloging-in-Publication Data:
Svetkey, Benjamin.
Leading man / by Benjamin Svetkey.—1st ed.
p. cm.
1. Young men—New York (State)—New York—Fiction.
2. Self-realization—Fiction. I. Title.
PS3619.V48   L43 2013
813'.6   2013002980

Vintage ISBN: 978-0-307-94961-5

Book design by Heather Kelly
Cover design by Abby Weintraub
Cover photograph © Alexander Yurinskiy/iStockphoto

www.vintagebooks.com

Printed in the United States of America
10   9   8   7   6   5   4   3   2   1

For Lenka and Chloe

ACKNOWLEDGMENTS

Thank you to my agent, Betsy Lerner, who, on more than one occasion, powered up the defibrillators and zapped this book back from the dead. Thank you to Claudia Herr, my editor at Vintage, and her colleague Peter Gethers, without whom this novel literally would not exist. Thank you to my friend Sean Smith, who spent part of his time in the Peace Corps last year e-mailing me literary guidance from a tin hut in Africa. Thank you to so many others, famous and unfamous, living and deceased, who helped me tell this story.

LEADING
MAN

1

(2005)

The knocking began at two in the morning. Three sharp raps, a few seconds of silence, then three more. I crawled out of bed, grabbed a fluffy robe from the bathroom—"Grand Hotel d'Angkor" it said in gold lettering on the breast pocket—and opened the door.

Nobody was there.

I didn't know a soul in Cambodia, certainly not anyone who'd pay a visit at this late hour, so I figured some other hotel guest must have mixed up a room number. I slid back into the comfy king-size bed with the eight-hundred-thread-count sheets, slipped on the eye mask from the minibar, switched off the light, and drifted back to sleep. A few minutes later, though, the knocking started again. Three raps, silence, three more. I headed to the door again. The hallway was still empty.

I don't believe in ghosts, but if any place seemed likely to be haunted, it was this hotel in Siem Reap. The village itself was straight out of a Children's Fund late-night TV spot. It was made up mostly of crumbling clay shacks and muddy streets, and the surrounding jungle was littered with unexploded land mines left over from Cambodia's on-again-off-again civil war. Beggars were everywhere, many of them small children. Buddhist monks in flowing orange robes flocked to the area too, drawn by the Zen magnetism of the nearby Temple of Angkor Wat, the super-sacred eight-hundred-year-old Buddhist shrine located a few miles down a dirt road. But smack in the middle of this twelfth-century landscape, sticking out like Lady Gaga at an ashram, was the five-star Grand Hotel d'Angkor, a colonial palace that had been catering to rich European tourists since Cambodia had been a French outpost back in the 1930s. This was about as far from Western civilization as you could get—in Siem Reap, elephants were still considered a form of mass transit—yet the doormen at the Grand Hotel all wore dainty white gloves.

I had ventured into Cambodia feeling like Captain Willard on the Nung River, in search of DeeDee Devry, the blond movie starlet famous for her in-your-face acting style, stunning violet eyes, and tumultuous private life. DeeDee—or Double-D, as she was nicknamed by the Hollywood press—was in Siem Reap shooting a high-concept action picture called *Time Tank*. She was starring as a U.S. Army tank commander in Afghanistan who takes a wrong turn into a temporal vortex that sends her and her vehicle hopscotching through portals in time and space. Think *Band of Brothers* meets *Bill & Ted's Excellent Adventure*. At one point in the script, there's a stop in medieval Indochina, where DeeDee's character is worshipped by the Khmer natives, the old blond-goddess-in-the-jungle routine.

Technically, I was a member of the Hollywood press, although I didn't spend a lot of time in Hollywood. My job was to fly around the world, interview movie stars and other celebrities, and write about them in the pages of KNOW magazine, the much-venerated, widely read news weekly headquartered in New York. It was a preposterously glamorous gig, the sort of jet-setting occupation a shallow Matthew McConaughey character might have in a cheesy romantic comedy—until McConaughey's character falls in love in the second act and learns the greater bliss of settling down with a regular girl like Kate Hudson. Only I was stuck in my second act. I was in my thirties and was unable to fall in love. The way things were going, I'd end up as Matthew McConaughey for the rest of my life, and nobody wants that.

It didn't matter what sort of girl I dated when I was back home in the United States—the punky music publicist with prematurely blue hair, the sexy sculptress who made spooky artwork out of glass eyeballs, the struggling actress who was so superstitious she dealt herself tarot cards before every audition—I always ended up running away. My intentions were honorable. I would go into each new romance with an open mind, hoping this would be the one that would stick, but it never did. Sooner or later, I would find deal-breaking flaws. A cackling laugh. Thick ankles. Loud chewing. And that was it, I would bolt. I knew, of course, I had plenty of flaws of my own, much worse than unshapely ankles. But I couldn't help myself.

Lucky for me, though, there was one type of relationship I was really good at—the kind I had with megafamous strangers. Who cared that I couldn't fall in love? Jack Nicholson knew my name! At least he did for the ninety minutes I spent with him in one of his mansions on Mulholland Drive. Who needed real intimacy with real people when fake intimacy with celebrities I would never see again was so much easier, so much fun? Unlike relationships with the unfamous—which often involved inconvenient emotions like longing or remorse—my relationships with stars were totally feeling-free. The rules of engagement were simple: I'd sit down with someone I'd never met and politely ask him or her invasive questions that would never come up in casual conversation—"What's it like getting busted with a hooker in your car?" "Why do people think your husband is gay?"—while the stars tried to charm and disarm me, revealing as little about themselves as possible. It was both an intensely personal and completely counterfeit form of communication. It's not how human beings are wired to interact. I loved it. To me, it was an entire romance, from seduction to betrayal, compressed into a single deadline.

And now I was in a hotel room in Southeast Asia, trying to get some sleep before meeting with yet another international superstar. Only some joker kept rapping on my door, then vanishing into thin air. I sat in bed and thumbed through some magazines. When I got bored with that, I grabbed the remote and turned on the TV. There were only two channels to watch in Cambodia, even at the Grand Hotel. One was broadcasting the *Asia Business Report* from Hong Kong. The other was airing a rerun of *Ally McBeal*. I killed a half hour watching Calista Flockhart dubbed in Taiwanese. When it was clear the knocker was not going to return, I switched off the light and curled back into a sleeping position.

A few minutes later, the knocking started again.

The Temple of Angkor Wat, where *Time Tank* was filming, is one of the most mystical places on Earth. It's an immense pile of ornately sculpted sandstone edifices that have been baking and crumbling in the scorching Cambodian heat for eight centuries. Its smooth stone floors are worn and cracked, and entire sections of the monument are missing, snatched away by Western tomb raiders a century ago. But its five gigantic pinecone-like spires remain untouched by time. They tower over the jungle skyline like an ancient, unsolved mystery—beehive hairdos of the gods.

When I arrived on the set the following morning, it looked as if a real army had invaded. Truckloads of video equipment had been unloaded, huge camera cranes had been erected, and trailers and tents had popped up all around the shrine. The scene they were shooting involved DeeDee's character being chased through the temple by outraged Khmer warriors, who had finally discovered that their new goddess was a mere mortal after all. To escape, she would have to jump from a twenty-foot wall into the jungle below (landing on an air mattress just out of camera range). On the screen, the leap would make up maybe three or four seconds of footage. But it would take all day to film.

There are rules when a journalist visits a movie set. You don't just waltz past the cameraman and start chatting with the stars. There are protocols to follow, pecking orders to observe. For starters, there's always a chaperone, or "unit publicist," to escort the press around the set. On *Time Tank,* that was Katherine Fust, a slightly discombobulated English woman who was having a tough time adjusting to the sweltering Cambodian climate. "I should have stayed in London," she complained, wilting in her Marks & Spencer safari outfit. "I could have been working on a Brendan Fraser movie!" Another rule: the star always sets the time and place for the interview. And the bigger the star, the longer the wait. In Cambodia, for instance, I figured it would be at least a couple of days before I'd get to sit down with Double-D. Meantime, I'd hang around the set, talk with the director and the lesser actors, and observe the actress at a discreet distance, until she summoned me to the interview. At least that's how it usually worked.

I had been on the set for only a couple of hours, just long enough to find a shady spot inside the temple where I could sit on the cool stone floor and close my jet-lagged eyes, when Katherine came rushing up to me. "I've been looking all over for you!" she said, sweaty and out of breath. "DeeDee wants to meet you. She wants to get a look at you before your interview. Which, by the way, she wants to do tomorrow." Katherine pointed to a lone canvas tent pitched about fifty yards from the temple, near the edge of the jungle. "She's in there," she said. "She's waiting for you. Now."

She was wearing a skin-tight tank commander uniform—in the world of *Time Tank*, the U.S. Army issued camouflage hot pants—with pneumatic enhancements that kept her magnificent chest cantilevered in front of her torso like the guns of Navarone. Strapped to a holster around her slender waist was a pair of pistols that looked like they could take down a rhino. But the costume was the least dazzling thing about her. Those eyes! Those lips! Those . . . eyes again! She was so gorgeous, so stunning to behold, I almost didn't hear what she was telling me. "There's a scorpion in here, is that going to bother you?" DeeDee was saying, as if apologizing for not tidying up before guests arrived. "He was over there," she said, nodding toward some sound equipment in the corner of the tent. "He must have moved. But he'll turn up eventually."

In magazine profiles, DeeDee was frequently described as "an old soul," which is Hollywood-speak for someone who's packed a lot of fast living into a very few years. Like a lot of kids born into the business—her dad was Leon Devry, the 1970s B-movie producer who gave David Lynch and Tim Burton their first crew jobs, and her mom was Yvette Vickers, the Playboy centerfold–turned–horror movie actress—she had a bumpy upbringing. Alcoholism, cocaine abuse, Vicodin addiction. And that was just middle school. As talented and committed an actress as she was—her portrayal of Tricia Nixon in the HBO drama

First Daughter won her a much-deserved Golden Globe—
she couldn't seem to step out of her own way. Married and
divorced twice—both times to the same rock musician—
she hit bottom at twenty-six, with a public mischief arrest
when police found her at five in the morning wading naked
in the fountain in front of the Dorothy Chandler Pavilion.
Now, at the ripe old age of twenty-eight, she was finally
clean and sober, and making a comeback with a movie
about a time-traveling M1A1 Abrams battle tank.

As I had my getting-to-know-you meeting with the
actress inside the scorpion-infested tent, I kept flinching,
imagining the tickle of arachnid feet on my skin. I wondered if DeeDee was testing me with this scorpion mind
game, or if she really could be that blasé about deadly
arthropods. I decided it was probably the latter. If you
were to draw a Venn diagram of "Hot" and "Crazy," Devry
would occupy the intersecting space smack in the middle.
"You know," she said, staring at my face, "you look a little like Paul Newman. Has anybody ever told you that?"
Sadly, no, nobody had. Probably because I looked nothing
like Paul Newman. With my shock of reddish brown hair
and cornflower blue eyes, I was more like Alfred E. Neu-
man. But this was an old trick movie stars played on journalists. It was intended to flatter and ingratiate, the way
politicians sometimes repeat a person's name after being
introduced. Kirsten Dunst once told me I looked like Paul
Bettany. Ashley Judd, weirdly, said I reminded her of her
cat. But DeeDee took the game a step further. She leaned
forward, pinched my chin between her thumb and forefin-
ger, and moved my head around as if examining a farm
animal. "Your eyes," she finally decided, "are definitely

Newman's. But you have Leo DiCaprio's chin." Then she flashed her famous DeeDee Devry grin.

The meeting lasted only a few minutes, until a production assistant peeked into the tent to announce that they were finally ready to start shooting the jump. For the next couple of hours, I watched the actress perform acrobatics in hundred-degree jungle heat. She dove off the temple wall (with body cables supporting her) over and over again, executing a perfect rolling landing every time. I couldn't take my eyes off her. And I wasn't the only one. Off in the distance, a line of orange figures stood atop another of the temple walls. Even the monks had come out to watch the blond goddess in action.

That night, the knocking started earlier, at about midnight. Again, there was nobody at the door. I threw on some clothes and headed to the hotel lobby.

"A knocking sound, you say?" asked the attendant at the front desk. He was a Cambodian man in his sixties with a French accent, and silver, slicked-back hair. A little gold nameplate on his jacket said "Nhean."

"Yeah, like somebody's at the door, but then nobody is," I explained.

"A knocking but with nobody there," Nhean repeated, as if he was having trouble understanding.

"Yes," I said. "I'd like to change rooms, please."

Nhean consulted his computer for a few moments, then frowned. "I'm so sorry, monsieur," he said. "We are completely filled. With all the movie people from Hollywood, we have no rooms left." He shrugged his shoulders.

"Well, has anybody else complained about knocking?" I asked. I was thinking that a mad late-night knocker might be running amok in the hotel, and that I was just one of his victims.

"Not that I am aware of," Nhean said. Then, after a pause, "Would you like me to accompany you to your room so that I can hear this knocking for myself?"

I shook my head no, yawned, and turned around to head back to my room. That's when I heard the jazzy tinkle of piano keys coming from the hotel lounge—the Elephant Bar, it was called, presumably because of all the polished tusks adorning the walls—and decided to pop in for a nightcap. Even at midnight, the place was hopping, with a dozen members of the *Time Tank* crew drinking and laughing as they lazed in oversize wicker armchairs and sofas. I spotted Katherine Fust drinking by herself in a corner of the bar. As a rule, I don't fraternize with unit publicists—they're usually too worried about saying something that could end up in print to be any fun as drinking buddies—but that didn't turn out to be a problem with Katherine.

"I hate my job," she said the minute I sat in the wicker chair next to her. "I hate my life." I took a long sip of my Airavata cocktail (a specialty of the Elephant Bar, made with rum, coconut juice, pineapple, and lots more rum) but I knew I'd need several more to catch up to Katherine. The publicist was smashed. "I'm sick of movie sets," she went on, not caring, or even much noticing, that she was talking to a journalist. "I'm sick of movie stars! Do you know what I had to do today? I had to find chocolate-covered Peeps in Cambodia. You know, those marshmallow candy things? One of the producers read somewhere that our leading lady is a freak for them. The fat fuck producer comes up to me and tells me that it's absolutely essential—those were his words, *absolutely essential*—that we have chocolate-covered Peeps in DeeDee's trailer by tomorrow. But guess what? There are no fucking Peeps in fucking Cambodia! As far as I can tell, there's no marshmallow-type candy of any kind in this whole fucking country. I had to call Los Angeles and have them put a box on a plane to Siem Reap. It's going to cost the production three thousand dollars. And you know what? I bet DeeDee doesn't even like them. I bet she's never even eaten one. But I'm going to get fired over fucking Peeps."

"I hate Peeps" was the most sympathetic thing I could think to say when Katherine finished talking. I had mostly stopped listening, anyway, and was concentrating instead on a pretty brunette at the bar, noticing how one strap of her camisole top was slipping down her slender shoulder. It's not that I didn't feel for Katherine. I knew she had one of those jobs that sounded great on paper—travel to exotic places with movie stars!—but in reality led to a slow corrosion of the soul. I had one of those jobs, too. But I was still jet-lagged and groggy, thanks to the knocking that was keeping me awake, and I didn't have the energy to cheer up a drunken publicist I barely knew. I was about to make up an excuse to get up from my chair when Katherine let out an enormous hiccup. "Fuck," the publicist said. Then she slumped down in her chair and passed out cold.

I thought about striking up a conversation with the brunette I'd been eyeing but a curly-haired guy in his twenties sat down next to her and they promptly began making out. I decided to return to my room. As soon as I got back I crawled into bed and was just about to switch off the light when a revelation hit me: the knocking occurred only in the dark. Whoever or whatever it was that had been banging on my door—a ghost, a prankster, a drunken hotel guest—it never happened when the lights were on. I tested my theory by switching off the bedside lamp. Sure enough, within minutes, the rapping resumed. When I turned the light back on, it stopped. I began to formulate a plan.

I put the bathrobe on again and headed back to the lobby. I borrowed a flashlight from Nhean—he didn't seem surprised to see me—and returned to my room. I turned off the light and waited in the dark. When the rapping started, I turned on the flashlight. Just as I'd hoped, it wasn't bright enough to chase away whatever was making the noise. I listened for a while, noticing how the rapping got louder and louder. I tried to follow the sound to its source. It was definitely coming from near the door, but, weirdly, from my side of it. And from above. I slowly raised the beam of light up the wall to the ceiling, until I saw . . . a small spotted lizard poking out from behind a light fixture. I stared at it for a few seconds. It stared back at me. Then it opened its mouth. Out came three sharp gecko barks that sounded exactly like someone knocking on a door.

"Oh, for Christ's sake," I said.

"Knock, knock, knock," the gecko repeated.

I rushed back to the hotel lobby one more time, excited to tell Nhean about my discovery. Also, I needed someone to come to my room to remove the lizard. "It is considered good luck!" Nhean explained after he heard the story. "It is a good sign to find one in your room!"

"Good luck?" I asked.

"Also, they eat the mosquitoes," Nhean said.

"What about the luck?" I asked.

"We call them Chhin Chhos," Nhean explained. "If you listen to what it is saying, you will have good luck. It is trying to tell you something, monsieur. But you must listen."

"Oh really," I said, a little sarcastically. I was starting to suspect that Nhean was pulling my leg. "And what would a lizard be telling me by making knocking noises at one a.m.?" It was a rhetorical question, but Nhean answered it anyway.

"I don't know, monsieur. Maybe it is saying, 'Wake up!'"

The next morning, DeeDee was shooting a scene in which she'd row a small canoe around a moat protecting the temple. In point of fact, there actually were ancient trenches surrounding the shrine, but most had been bone-dry for centuries. Thanks to Hollywood magic—a fleet of water-pumping trucks—it took only a couple of days to get them filled up again.

Amazingly, it was even hotter on day two of my set visit, and Katherine the publicist looked even more miserable. "I could be in Prague right now," she complained, fanning herself with her safari hat. "I could be working on a Johnny Depp movie!" Remarkably, she didn't seem to have any memory of our conversation in the Elephant Bar the night before.

To help people deal with the heat, production assistants handed out bandannas that had been soaking in tubs of ice water, which the film crew tied around their foreheads like little air-conditioning units. It made the set resemble a Bruce Springsteen look-alike convention, but I joined in and put one on, too. Even DeeDee seemed to be melting in the heat. When she climbed out of the canoe after she finished filming her rowing scene, I spotted a few dewy drops of perspiration rolling down her neck toward her cleavage. The actress whispered some words to her director, then, surprisingly, headed straight for me. More celebrity interview convention: stars don't directly approach reporters on a set. If they want to talk to one, they send a publicist or some other underling to beckon him. But this star took matters into her own hands. "I'm almost ready for our interview," she said as she wrapped a chilled bandanna around her brow. "Why don't you meet me in my trailer in about twenty minutes? It's air-conditioned. It'll be more comfortable."

The air was cooler in the trailer, that much was true, but it was hardly more comfortable. On the contrary, I'd never perspired so much in my life. When I arrived at DeeDee's Star Waggon twenty minutes later, as requested, the actress opened the door wearing nothing but a sheer, soaking-wet bedsheet. "Just stepped out of the shower," she explained. "Hope you don't mind." She sat down on a sofa inside the trailer and crossed her legs, the soaked sheet falling open to reveal a stretch of upper thigh. Then she smiled and offered to answer any question I cared to ask, once I regained the power of speech.

There were three possibilities for what was going on here. One, the star was trying to seduce me. I thought this highly unlikely. After all, I was a lowly reporter, one or two notches above grip in the social hierarchy of a movie set. Two, the actress was cynically attempting to manipulate a member of the press by using her body as a distraction and diversion. I thought this a distinct possibility. Or three, DeeDee was simply a free spirit who didn't care that the air-conditioning in her trailer was making her nipples stand out under the translucent bedsheet like No. 2 pencil erasers. That was plausible, too.

I did the best interview I could under the circumstances. But it took all my concentration just to maintain eye contact, let alone remember my questions. I asked the star about her latest tattoo ("My body is my home—I like to decorate it," she answered). I asked about her second split from her first husband ("It's true what they say," she said, "divorce is more wonderful the second time around"). At one point, I noticed a shark tooth pendant on a thin gold chain around her neck, so I asked about that. "This," she said, "is my good luck charm. I never take it off. I feel *nude* without it." She thrust out her chest to offer a closer look, all but smothering my face in her décolletage. "Don't you think it's the most beautiful thing you've ever seen?" she purred. I tried to answer, but all that came out of my mouth was a plaintive squeak.

Later in the interview, though, after my breathing returned to normal, something even more surprising happened. I found myself fixated on parts of DeeDee's body that weren't erogenous zones. Oddly, I found myself staring at her arms. They were, I couldn't help but notice, veiny. You sometimes see it with weight lifters and bodybuilders—low body fat and excessive working out make the veins expand to pump more oxygen to the extremities. DeeDee had obviously been overexercising. She had blood vessels as thick as Twizzlers bulging from her elbows to her wrists. Smaller capillaries made unsightly blue spiderwebs on her biceps. Frankly, it was a real turnoff. Also, what was up with that birthmark on her hip that I could almost see peeking through the wet bedsheet? Or was that another tattoo? Either way, I found it strangely repulsive. How come I hadn't noticed any of these things before? Okay, I knew how come, but now that I had noticed I couldn't stop looking.

Yes, that's right, I was alone in a trailer with a beautiful, nearly naked movie star. I was being shown skin not meant for mortal eyes. I was living the fantasy of a million male moviegoers. And what did I focus on? The same thing I always focused on whenever I found myself attracted to a woman—her flaws. Her big, veiny, deal-breaking flaws. "What the hell is wrong with me?" I wondered as I stepped out of DeeDee's trailer an hour later, gasping for air and soaked in sweat.

2

I wasn't born an intimacy-phobic, fame-obsessed a-hole. Nobody ever is. It requires a powerful transformative event to do that sort of damage to a man's psyche. In this case, the story begins with a lifelong love affair with a superhero.

I adored Johnny Mars from the moment I laid eyes on him. Of all the eighties action stars of my youth, he was the one I idolized most. I would have given anything to be him, or just a little bit more like him. Sardonic and suave. Dashingly ruthless. A smooth maneuver around every danger, a clever comeback for every situation. Who could forget his classic line in *Give Me Death,* delivered in his trademark growl, just before his famous FBI agent character, Jack Montana, blows away the bad guy on the steps of the Lincoln Memorial ("Glory, glory, hallelujah, douchebag!"). Or that scene in *Live Free or Kill,* when Montana pushes an assassin out of the landing-gear hatch of Air Force One ("Have a nice flight, dickweed!").

I couldn't forget them, but then I was still a twelve-year-old boy long after I grew up.

And then Johnny Mars stole my girlfriend.

If this book were a movie, right about now everything would get all wavy as we dissolved to a flashback of New York City circa 1994. Dennis Franz is baring buttocks on *NYPD Blue*. Kurt Cobain is making flannel a fashion statement. Rudy Giuliani is cracking down on jaywalking during his first term as mayor. And I, a rookie reporter in my twenties, am heading for a newsstand near the subway entrance on Sixth Avenue in Greenwich Village, just as I did every morning on the way to work. We are approaching the precise moment in time when my world shatters. The moment I learn that my girlfriend—my true love, the woman I planned to marry, the one who was supposedly spending the summer redefining the role of Anya in a production of *The Cherry Orchard* at the prestigious Concord Theater Festival up in Massachusetts—has left me for the movie star I worshipped throughout my childhood. And adulthood too.

My first clue came from the *New York Post*. As you can imagine, it was subtle. MARS OVER THE MOON! announced a headline on Page Six, above a picture of the hulking actor with his arm around a woman who looked amazingly like my own beloved Samantha. According to the article, the forty-two-year-old superstar had fallen for my twenty-four-year-old girlfriend during rehearsals for *The Cherry Orchard*. Mars was always trying to prove that he was a real actor, capable of playing parts that didn't involve battling parasailing terrorists over the Grand Canyon, so he had muscled his way into the part of Lopakhin in

Concord's production of the Chekhov classic. According to the *Post*, Samantha and Mars had been a "hot item" for several weeks, which would explain the recent lack of phone calls from Sammy. Still, I figured this must be a mistake. I bought a copy of the more reliable *Daily News*. There was an item in that paper too. Mars, it said, was "swooning" over his new "gal pal," and was planning on moving her into his Upper West Side penthouse when the festival ended and the couple returned to New York the following week. Getting desperate, I purchased *The New York Times*. Even the Old Gray Lady was spreading the news. A profile of Mars in the Arts section included a reference to the fact that "Mr. Mars" had become "romantically involved" with one of the actresses at the festival, "a Ms. Samantha Kotter, originally from Westchester."

Suddenly, it seemed like the asphalt on Sixth Avenue had turned to rubber. My legs went wobbly and my heart started pounding, and there was something wrong with my stomach, too. I felt like I'd been whacked in the gut with a large carnival mallet.

Samantha and I had been childhood sweethearts. We met in seventh grade when Sammy spotted me on the playground and introduced herself by whipping a snowball at my head. "Hey," twelve-year-old Samantha said as she watched me brush the stinging ice from my eyes. "You're standing on my snow."

"Your snow?" I replied, confused, mostly by the fact that a girl was talking to me.

"I was going to build a snowman where you're standing, but you've ruined the snow. You got your footprints all over."

"It's not ruined," I argued, stepping gingerly from the spot. "You can still make a snowman."

"Well then," Samantha said, "you'd better help."

And so it began, our decades-long love affair. From then on, Samantha would have an above-the-title role in my life. She would become the first girl I took to the movies. The first to hold my hand. The first to let me kiss her. Every first there was to have, I had with her. Every second, third, and fourth, too.

By our early twenties, we were living together in an L-shaped studio on the fourth floor of a rent-controlled apartment building on a cobblestone street in the West Village. It had a refrigerator that gave an electric shock whenever you touched its handle, and the walls would shake whenever a truck rumbled past the window, but I loved the place. In the morning we could hear birds chirping outside. At night, we could hear the *cloppity-clop* of police horses on the cobblestones—and also the screeches of transsexual hookers from the nearby Meatpacking District. A freshly minted journalism degree in hand, I had landed my first magazine job. Each day I would jump on the subway uptown to Fiftieth Street, and all but jog a couple of blocks to the glass tower where *KNOW*'s headquarters were located, on the top floor overlooking Times Square. As a new staff writer, the junior-most scribe, I had a small windowless office next to the men's room. But it was my own office all the same, with my own name—Maxwell Lerner—stenciled on the door. When I first stepped inside and sat down behind my desk (my own desk!), I knew exactly how Melanie Griffith felt at the end of *Working Girl*.

Samantha, meanwhile, was busy auditioning for acting roles. At twenty-four, she was a walking David Hamilton photograph, a fresh-faced poster child for natural beauty, with big brown doe eyes and a mane of silky brunette hair that dangled just above her waistline. She was also a gifted actress and singer. Still, at first the only work she could find was in a children's theater in Murray Hill. Every night she would arrive back home with her face smeared in clown paint. I would huddle with her over the bathroom sink and gently remove her makeup. Sometimes I'd make jokes about the rubber clown nose.

"Maybe you could leave this on tonight," I teased, arching an eyebrow.

"Acting is so glamorous." Samantha ignored me, staring dejectedly at her reflection in the mirror. "My next part will probably be a dancing cupcake."

"You'd make an incredibly sexy cupcake," I said, nuzzling her neck, getting clown paint all over my chin.

"You don't get famous by playing cupcakes." Samantha sighed, examining her teeth in the mirror.

Then it happened: Samantha got her big break in *The Cherry Orchard*. And she headed up to Concord for the summer, where she finally got famous, although not exactly for her acting. I couldn't believe how ironic it all was. When I first learned that Samantha would be sharing the stage with Johnny Mars at the festival, I couldn't have been more thrilled, and made several unsubtle hints about wanting to meet the guy whose action figures I'd obsessively collected as a kid. Sammy was not as impressed. "I might as well be doing Shakespeare with Arnold Schwarz-enegger," she complained. "Or Molière with Sylves-ter Stallone." By the end of the summer, Samantha had apparently had a change of heart. She was now Johnny Mars's number one fan. And I hated his guts.

I got a dollar's change from the newsstand guy on Sixth Avenue and looked around for a pay phone. There was no answer when I called Sammy in Concord—just her normal, faithful-sounding voice on the answering machine—so I hung up and continued on to work. I spent the morning sitting at my desk staring at the wall, absorb-ing the hit I'd taken. During my lunch break, while poking at my uneaten sandwich in a deli, I told my coworker and soon-to-be best friend, Robin, what had happened. A lot of clever wags worked at *KNOW,* but Robin, the recep-tionist, was the wittiest of them all. She was a pretty Ital-ian girl with soulful green eyes and long dark hair—sort of like Mona Lisa's younger, lesbian sister—but she had all the sensitivity of an insult comic. "Wow, that's rough," she said. "How can you compete with Johnny Mars? He's rich. He's famous. He's beloved by millions. He's so hand-some even *I'd* consider sleeping with him." She paused for a second. "Are you going to eat that pickle?"

Of course, Robin was right. I couldn't compete with Johnny Mars—as his number one fan for years, I knew that better than anyone. But that's not what hurt the most. What stung worse was the fact that I learned the details of my cuckolding from the newspapers. Losing a girlfriend to a celebrity wasn't just humiliating—it was *publicly* humiliating. Everybody knew about it. That eve-ning, when I returned home after work, even my landlady made a point of stopping me at the stairwell to giddily show me the item on Page Six linking my former soul mate—her ex-tenant—with a movie star. People can't help but be excited when somebody they've known in their everyday lives suddenly becomes famous, even if it's just for dating someone famous. It's the fairy tale, and you can't help but root for fairy tales. To my landlady, hell, even to me, it made Samantha loom larger than life, lifted her into a VIP world full of stretch limos and film premieres and paparazzi flashbulbs. And I, the unfamous, heartbroken ex-boyfriend, had been left behind, my nose pressed up against the window just like everyone else's.

Samantha must have known that I had learned about her and Mars. Paparazzi shots of the two of them had even made the local TV news that night. There were several messages from Sam on the answering machine when I entered my apartment. "Are you there, Max? I really need to talk to you." I listened to Sammy's voice on the tape as I stared at a pair of her crumpled pantyhose at the bottom of our closet. "I'll be back in New York in a couple of days," she said, "but I really need to talk to you now. I'm so sorry. Please call me back, *please*."

I didn't call her back. Instead, I unplugged the phone and turned off the answering machine. I had asked Robin not to tell anyone at the office, but the story was everywhere, and I was sure the other *KNOW* writers had already propped a cardboard Johnny Mars standup in my chair, and had plans for plenty more jokes designed to remind me that the woman I loved was now sleeping in a movie star's bed. *KNOW* writers were clever that way. So for the next few days, I called in sick, stayed home, and tried to cheer myself up. I destroyed old photographs with a Magic Marker, drawing villainous mustaches and devil horns on Samantha's face. When that didn't work, I tried throwing out her stuff, the acting books and bottles of moisturizer and whatever clothing she hadn't taken with her to Concord. But some things I just couldn't part with, let alone deface. There was a photograph of Samantha at sixteen, a big, sweet grin on her face as she stood in a snowy patch of woods wearing the too-large fisherman's sweater I had given her for Christmas. I put the cap back on the Magic Marker when I came to that picture. And there was that green ceramic turtle Samantha had made in a fourth-grade pottery class that she kept on our kitchen table—I couldn't bring myself to destroy that, either. It was just two pinch pots stuck together with a dollop of clay for a head and a slot for saving coins on top, but I really liked that turtle.

Samantha and I fell in love at such young, impressionable ages, it seemed to me as if we had molded each other out of clay. My values, my tastes, my fears, my dreams— Samantha was there, at ground zero, to help form them all. Sure, we had our spats. Samantha sometimes complained that I was self-centered and self-involved. She was right, of course. I was a guy in my twenties. "You don't *listen* to me," Samantha complained one night as I was reorganizing my CD collection. She'd come home upset about a bad audition—at least I think that's what she was upset about—but I was too preoccupied trying to figure out where my new Deep Forest album belonged, in the World Music section or Ambient Dub, to pay much attention. "Max, you're always in your own universe," Sammy complained. "Doesn't it ever get lonely in there?"

My forgetfulness about birthdays and anniversaries became a running joke between us. But the longer it ran, the less funny it became. When I did remember, I put a lot of thought into the gifts I gave Sammy—just the wrong sort of thought. I never stopped to ask myself what she might want but instead got her presents I thought she should have. Or that I thought I should have. I'll never forget the bewildered, disappointed look on her face when she tore open the wrapping on a Christmas gift to uncover the laser disc box set of the complete *Man from U.N.C.L.E.* TV series. What girl wouldn't love thirty hours of a vintage spy show produced for twelve-year-old boys in the 1960s? "It's *so* great," I said, trying to cheer her up. "Really, you'll thank me later."

Even worse than buying her thoughtless presents, or forgetting her birthday altogether, or the time I decided to boycott Valentine's Day (a sham holiday concocted by the greeting card industry) was the fact that it never crossed my mind for a second that any of this stuff mattered. I was so certain that Samantha would love me forever, that she was the girl I was destined to marry and grow old with, that I ended up taking her totally for granted. No wonder I didn't notice the warning signs that were, during those final few months, flashing all over the place. When Samantha waved away my idea of taking the train up to Concord for a weekend visit, it didn't occur to me to be suspicious ("Rehearsals are so boring," she told me. "Besides, we wouldn't have much time to spend together—we're working round the clock"). The fact that Samantha's phone calls had dwindled from once a day when she first got to Concord to once a week, to none, didn't register as a red flag with me, either. Even if I had noticed, the idea that I might lose her, that she might be falling for someone else, was utterly unthinkable. There was nothing on Earth I was more sure of.

Until I read in the papers that I had it all wrong.

A few days later, I plugged my phone back in. It was time, I decided, to face the music. The phone rang almost immediately, but it wasn't Sammy. "You're coming tonight, right? You *are* coming." It was Robin calling; she was talking about a *KNOW* party that was being thrown that evening.

Every couple of months, *KNOW* threw a promotional event at one of the hot New York nightclubs. This was back when subscriptions were booming and the magazine industry was still in a partying mood. It was also the tail end of the clubbing era, when places like Nell's and Limelight were still so cool even people who lived on the Manhattan side of the bridges and tunnels would wait on line to get in. The lines were especially long when *KNOW* threw a party, with mobs of photographers pushing at the doors to get in. (Guests at *KNOW*'s bashes ran the gamut from supermodels to secretaries of state.) Best of all, the magazine's staffers had insta-passes to the center of the bacchanal. We got to stroll past the crowds, pinch the noses of the gorillas guarding the velvet rope, and saunter straight on into the club. Still, I wasn't feeling much like socializing.

"Oh c'mon!" Robin moaned into the phone. "It'll be

fun. Maybe you can steal some movie star's girlfriend. I hear Jim Carrey might show up tonight. You can leave with his plus one."

The idea of going home with anyone other than Samantha made me sick to my stomach. Not that I could get a movie star's girlfriend to talk to me, let alone leave a party with me. But I couldn't stay holed up in my studio apartment for the rest of my life. And I knew Robin wasn't going to take no for an answer.

There was a guy playing show tunes with a pair of spoons and some water glasses—*KNOW* always arranged "kooky" acts to entertain its guests—as well as about three hundred revelers drinking and dancing. The club was in an ancient brick building on Twenty-fifth Street—a century earlier, it had probably been a textile factory filled with child laborers—that had been gutted and converted into a multilevel hipster paradise. Every dimly lit floor was decorated with pool tables and leather Le Corbusier loungers.

Jim Carrey wasn't there, but I spotted a slew of other, lesser celebrities. I saw Jeremy Irons chatting with Gary Sinise at the bar. I saw Linda Evangelista and Helena Christensen scarfing down shrimp at the seafood buffet. I saw Kyle MacLachlan and Dan Hedaya standing on the same line for the men's room. Years later, after I became a more seasoned entertainment writer, I'd attend Hollywood parties that would make this one look as lame as a *Real World* reunion. But at the time, a close encounter with any celebrity, even Dan Hedaya, seemed new and exotic to me. It was at this party, and others like it, that I first came to the realization that the famous were different from you and me. In fact, I began to suspect that they weren't even the same species. They seemed to exist in a whole different dimension, a mesmerizing, alien world filled with bursting flashbulbs and bustling red carpets and vastly superior bone structure.

The world Sammy had just moved into.

I wandered through the club, observing famous creatures for a while. Then, at the bar, I ran into Ernie Moore, one of the few stars at the party I actually did know. I had interviewed the intense young Method actor just a month earlier, over lunch in SoHo, for a 150-word article on a Montgomery Clift bio-pic he was about to start shooting. It was my biggest story at *KNOW* so far; mostly I'd been getting assigned fifty-word obituaries on retired financiers and diplomats for the Endings page. But when one of the entertainment writers got stomach flu, I was asked to fill in at the last minute, like an understudy getting a big break. There wasn't enough light in the nightclub to read a wristwatch but, true to form, Moore was wearing a pair of dark sunglasses. "Hi!" I said, extending a friendly hand. "Nice to see you again." Moore peered over his eyewear. "And you are . . . ?" I'd yet to learn this cruel lesson: No matter how many hours you spend with a celebrity, no matter how many glowing things you say about them in print, they almost never remember you. To the famous, journalists are as nameless and faceless as the back of a cab driver's head.

This seemed like a good time to make my exit. I was

looking around for Robin to say good night when the crowd started to surge and thicken. Suddenly, I found myself pressed in among a sea of bodies. The doorman must have lost control, because photographers had broken the barricades and were now inside the club, elbowing through the masses with their clunky cameras. Slowly, I started working my way toward the exit, trying not to think of headlines like NIGHTCLUB CRUSH KILLS CELEBS (AND OTHERS). But just as I was about to make my getaway, I spotted the one celebrity I really didn't want to see. It was Johnny Mars, grinning and nodding to the throng as his bodyguards cleared a path in my direction. Hanging on his arm was the one person I didn't want to see more— Sammy. I had to get out of there, but the paparazzi were going wild setting off an explosion of blinding camera flashes. I was trapped by the crowd, being swept ever closer to the hot new couple.

Sammy spotted me before I could get away. I saw her whisper something in Johnny's ear and slip out of his protective circle toward me. "I'm so sorry, Max," she said, grabbing my arm to keep me from running away. "I know I should have told you earlier. I tried to tell you so many times." She squeezed my wrist and looked for any sign of understanding. "It wasn't like I planned it," she said. "It just happened. He kept sending me these flowers, and then . . ."

Had I been given the chance, I like to think I would have responded maturely. It's possible Sammy and I might have cheerfully clinked martini glasses and merrily chatted about old times, like characters in a Noël Coward comedy. Then again, I might have reacted more like

Brando in *Streetcar,* tearing at my T-shirt and bellowing at Samantha with brutish contempt. I'll never know. Before I could utter a word, a bunch of photographers popped up out of nowhere and started snapping Samantha's picture. "Johnny's looking for you," they badgered her between snaps. "Who's this guy? Why are you talking to him?" When it became clear the photographers weren't leaving, Samantha gave my arm another squeeze, mouthed the words "I'm sorry," and turned to rejoin her movie star boyfriend. For a minute, one of the paparazzi continued shooting pictures of me. Another pap grabbed him by the arm. "Forget it—he's nobody," he said over his shoulder as he ran after Samantha.

3

It'd be all too easy to draw a connection between Samantha's love affair with a movie star and my decision to pursue a career as an entertainment journalist. So let's get it over with.

As a junior writer at *KNOW*, I hadn't yet been given a section assignment. I might have ended up pursuing a spot in the magazine's Politics or Crime pages—those were the macho places to hang one's byline. I could see myself as a dashing, trench-coated journo ducking past police tape to report on a grisly murder scene, or maybe as a sophisticated foreign correspondent attending black-tie diplomatic soirees at the Palais de l'Élysée. But after Sammy left me, writing about celebrities took on a certain sadomasochistic appeal. Fame had snatched Sammy away from me, but I would keep her in my life by making fame my beat. I would chase after her as a member of the Hollywood media.

To be honest, though, I might well have ended up writing about movie stars even if Samantha hadn't fallen for one of them. From the moment I emerged from the womb, I've been an obsessive-compulsive pop culture junkie. I spent so many hours in front of my family's massive color Zenith that I absorbed enough radiation to power a Polaris submarine. It didn't matter if it was a classic Hitchcock movie or an episode of *Petticoat Junction*—if it was on TV, I watched it. I not only memorized TV theme song lyrics but could recite credits from the closing crawls of sitcoms like *Bewitched* and *Get Smart* (I knew, for instance, that Botany 500 did men's wardrobe for both). When I wasn't watching TV, I was devouring pulpy spy novels (all of Ian Fleming's during eighth grade, most of Alistair MacLean's during ninth), cracking up to the Bill Cosby comedy albums I found in my father's collection (until I started buying my own Richard Pryor records), and grooving to Duran Duran on my first Walkman. It was the ideal preparation for a future calling as an entertainment writer.

I grew up in suburban Shady Hill, New York—on the other side of the commuter tracks from Scarsdale—in a house that looked like it belonged on TV. The kitchen, with its lime-green linoleum countertops and daisy-themed wallpaper, could have been Carol Brady's. The tastefully bland living room furniture might have been picked out by Rob and Laura Petrie—there was even an awkwardly placed ottoman—and the den could have been designed by Ward Cleaver. I had an attic room over the garage, just like the Fonz, although for some reason, girls didn't come when I snapped my fingers.

My father, an ad exec at a Madison Avenue firm, was a charming, funny, Fred MacMurray–style dad who always made a point of affectionately ruffling my hair when he got home from work. Mom was a former beauty queen from Brooklyn whose knockout smile had once appeared in a toothpaste ad in *Life* magazine. They were as bright and breezy as any sixties sitcom couple, and just as sweetly corny. One of my earliest memories is watching my parents dancing to music from a transistor radio as they cleaned up together after a dinner party—how my mother laughed when my father dipped her over the sink, dunking her ponytail into the suds. And then, suddenly, without the slightest bit of TV-drama-style foreshadowing, there was the accident that turned our household into a tragic movie of the week.

I was eight years old at the time. I was sitting cross-legged in our den watching *Planet of the Apes* on Channel 7 when I noticed my dad standing by the door, looking stricken. He sat down in front of me on the floor, blocking the TV, and talked in halting, confusing sentences about a trip to the supermarket and brake failure and red lights. I wanted to see what was happening on the TV set. It was the part of the film when the gorillas snare Charlton Heston in a net and he stuns them by finally speaking—"Take your filthy paws off me, you damn dirty apes!" My dad finally spat out the words: my mom had been killed in a car crash.

Dad was never the same. He tried his best to raise me on his own. There were grim outings to Carvel for ice cream, where I would gorge myself while watching him stare into space, his cone melting untouched in his big fist. There were birthday parties, afternoons at ballparks, and all the other moments a boy is expected to accumulate during the course of a normal American childhood. But for most of it, my father was absent, even when he was standing right there. So I disappeared into my pop culture world, clinging to TV and movies for warmth and companionship. And predictability. Every week, no matter what else was going on around me, I could always count on Jan to get jealous of Marcia. I knew for sure that Gilligan would screw up and they wouldn't get rescued from the island. Somehow, at the end of the half hour, everything would be okay again, back to normal, everyone happy.

And then, in 1982, when I was twelve years old, while standing on the playground at school, I got smacked in the side of the head with a snowball.

Samantha lived only six blocks from my house, on a cheery tree-lined street called Cedar Lane. Her home couldn't have been more different from mine. While my house had become as gloomy as a James Agee novel, Sammy's was as wacky as a Kaufman and Hart screwball comedy. During dinner, Samantha and her two sisters juggled three conversations at once, like verbal plate spinners, diving in and out of the kitchen to help Sam's mom with a stove-top emergency, while Sammy's dad tossed scraps from his plate to the dog. The chaos didn't stop there. Samantha's room upstairs looked like it'd been hit by a tornado, followed by an A-bomb. Half-read paperbacks were splayed around the floor, homework poked out from under the covers of her old-fashioned sleigh bed, girly undergarments were stuffed under the cushion of a chair. On a bookshelf, half hidden by an empty box of Mallomars, was that ceramic turtle she had made in fourth grade.

One day when we were about fifteen, we were loung-ing on the lumpy mattress in her room reading maga-zines and listening to the radio when Samantha made an announcement. "I've decided that I'm going to become an actress," she said. This made sense. Samantha was an actress even before she knew she wanted to be an actress. But then she went on. "And I've decided that you should become a writer." I was accustomed to Sam's pronounce-ments. Just a year earlier, she had declared that it was time I got promoted from her best friend to her boyfriend. She grabbed my head as if picking up a melon and gave me my first kiss. I knew once Samantha made up her mind about something, it was pointless to argue. But I was curious.

"Why do you think I should be a writer?" I asked her.

"Because writers are interesting," she answered. "And writers and actresses make super-interesting couples. Like Marilyn Monroe and Henry Miller."

"Arthur Miller," I corrected her. "Henry Miller's the one who had the affair with Anaïs Nin—remember that book of hers I showed you?"

"Or Lillian Hellman and Raymond Chandler . . ."

"It was Dashiell Hammett. And Lillian Hellman was a writer, too, not an actress."

"Whoever. The point is, I'm going to be a famous actress, so you have to become a famous writer. That way we can be famous together for the rest of our lives." She peered up from a magazine and gave me a smile. "You bet-ter start writing, buster."

Samantha wasn't kidding. She threw herself into drama classes and auditioned for every high school musical. She began reading Uta Hagen and would torture me with Meisner Technique acting exercises (she once spent an entire day repeating the phrase, "How could you?" inflected in every variation imaginable). As for my part of the deal, I enjoyed the idea of being a writer a whole lot more than the actual paperwork. I liked to imagine myself as a Fleming-esque figure, tapping out twisty spy novels on a manual typewriter as I swigged martinis and chain-smoked unfiltered cigarettes. But whenever I actually sat down to try to write something for real, I'd end up drawing doodles of Marvin the Martian. I knew early on that my true calling wasn't as an author. It was as Samantha's audience.

When the time came, we went away to different colleges, although we made sure we didn't stray too far apart. I ended up in New Hampshire, Samantha in Vermont. It was only a couple of hours between campuses. Still, we made the most of the drama of our separation. From the long, mopey letters we mailed each other, you'd think we'd been imprisoned on opposite ends of the universe. After graduation, it was Samantha's idea that we move together to New York. She had prodded me to major in journalism in college—one way or another, she was going to make a writer out of me—and she pushed me to apply for that job at *KNOW*. Sammy picked our studio in the West Village, chose the fold-out sofa bed we bought from a furniture shop on Eighth Street, and decided what take-out dishes to order from the Chinese restaurant around the corner, but I kept the most important power for myself.

I had final say on the video we'd rent from the store on Hudson Street.

When Sammy got accepted to the Concord Theater Festival, I took her out to an Italian restaurant on Perry Street and ordered an $8 bottle of champagne. We toasted her future and I joked about her not remembering me after she got famous. Later that night, we brought a quart of Häagen-Dazs chocolate ice cream into the sofa bed with us and watched the video I'd chosen for the evening's entertainment. It was *A Hard Day's Night*. At one point, John Lennon picks up a guitar and starts casually strumming a tune. "If I fell in love with you," he sings, "would you promise to be true . . ." Sammy put her head on my shoulder, licked a scoop of Häagen-Dazs, and passed the spoon back to me.

I never saw Johnny Mars coming.

4

Interviewing celebrities is not as easy as it looks. It's a delicate process, not unlike coaxing a frightened kitten out from under a bed. To get them to purr into a tape recorder, you have to talk to them in soft, nonthreatening tones. Plenty of ego-stroking is a good idea, too. It establishes trust. Whatever you do, avoid asking questions that require any serious thinking. You don't want to startle them.

I learned all this the hard way, by trial and lots of error.

It's not like they gave me an instruction manual when I moved over to the entertainment beat at *KNOW* shortly after Samantha ran off, taking my will to live with her. It was presumed that I was already aware of how to do my job, otherwise why would such an esteemed magazine have hired me? Actually, I had no idea how to do my job. Fortunately, the editor of the Entertainment section didn't seem to know what she was doing, either. As far as I could tell, Carla Dreysdale devoted virtually all her time and energy to collecting and playing with the dozens and dozens of snow globes that filled every surface of her sleek corner office. We're not simply talking about Welcome to Miami–style souvenir globes, although there were plenty of those. We're talking about rare globes from obscure East European cities, a Spiro Agnew snow globe from the 1968 presidential race, even an antique prop snow globe that was used as a stand-in for the most famous snow globe in all of snow globe history—the one Orson Welles lets out of his hand at the end of *Citizen Kane*. That precious collector's item got a special place of honor in Carla's office, a spotlit bookshelf all its own, presumably protected by motion-detecting laser alarms when she shut the lights off and left for the day.

The other writers at *KNOW* weren't much help to me, either. They were always either flying off on some assignment or barricaded behind their office doors playing Beat the Clock with their deadlines. Some writers never turned up at the office at all; they'd file their stories from Berlin or Budapest, or wherever they happened to be. Then there were a couple who never seemed to leave. This one guy in the Religion section—the Stone Cutter was his nickname—had been locked in his office working on the same piece about fake first editions in the Vatican Library for nearly two years. I wasn't about to ask him for career advice. About the only person I could turn to was Robin, the receptionist, who actually did offer me some pretty good guidance. "Speak to celebrities as if they were normal people and speak to normal people as if they were celebrities," she suggested over lunch. "That's what I do when I answer the phones. Seems to work pretty well. Are you going to eat those chips?" We became friends fast.

Not surprisingly, I made plenty of rookie mistakes. Like when the magazine sent me on my first trip to Los Angeles for a story on *Star Flight*, the long-running TV space opera about an interstellar battleship marooned in a distant galaxy, and I almost got kicked off the set. It was the first time I'd ever stepped foot inside a Hollywood soundstage, and I found myself so starstruck my jaw actually dropped. There it was, in the flesh, so to speak, the iconic bridge of the USS *Ultimatum*, the spaceship I'd been fantasizing about since I was ten. The cast and crew were on lunch break, the unit publicist had ducked out to take a phone call, and I was all alone. Naturally, I climbed into the captain's chair. How could I resist? But before my butt hit the seat, production assistants came running from all over the stage, shouting and waving their arms. Sitting on the captain's space lounger, it turned out, was strictly forbidden.

"Oh my God!" the unit publicist shrieked when she returned from her phone call and found out what I'd almost done. "That's the captain's chair! Are you insane?"

That day I learned Rule No. 1: Don't ever, under any circumstances, touch anything on a soundstage, no matter how irresistible the temptation. A little later on, thanks to a slightly more awkward lesson, I learned Rule No. 2: Don't ever, under any circumstances, no matter how irresistible the temptation, ask an aging starlet about her penis.

It'd been eight months since I started at *KNOW*. Carla called me into her office with an assignment. "You'll like this story," she said as she unpacked a box with her latest acquisition, a snow globe with a miniature Monrovian village inside. "It's a one-page profile of Sissy Skye. Remember her?" Sure did. She was before my time, but I knew her work. In the late 1960s Skye had the most famous hairdo on planet Earth, a sort of shaggy Veronica Lake–like thing that fell fetchingly over half her face, covering one eye. It was smoldering and sexy. It was also, famously, responsible for one of the biggest hair-related crazes ever to sweep the nation, and probably countless mishaps in junior high school hallways as millions of fourteen-year-old girls stumbled to classes half-blinded by bangs. Even if I hadn't known who Skye was, though, I would have jumped at the assignment. A one-page story in *KNOW* magazine was a huge opportunity. That was at least four hundred words!

"You know about the rumor, right?" Carla went on, giving her new globe a little shake. "Of course you do—everybody knows about the rumor. I want you to try to get her to talk about it. She's never said anything on the record about it before—maybe she's finally ready. If you can get her to talk about it, there's a chance we could bump the story up to a two-pager."

"Okay," I said, pretending to know what Carla was talking about. "I'll make sure to get into that with her. Ask about the rumor. You betcha."

"You know," Carla added, putting down the globe and looking me straight in the eye, "if you can get Skye to open up about this, there's even a chance of a cover line."

Later, when I asked Robin what the rumor was, I was astonished to learn that people had been gossiping for years about Sissy Skye's anatomical origins. It was an open secret—according to Robin—that Skye had been born with infantile hermaphroditism, and that surgery had been required to make her fully female. It explained, Robin said, why Skye had never had children, even though she'd been married three times. If I could get the actress to talk about all this, delve into her genital history, as it were, Carla had all but promised me a cover line. I had to try.

And so I flew to Hollywood to ask Sissy Skye if she had been born with a penis. We met for lunch at the Polo Lounge in Beverly Hills. It was a favorite hot spot for maturing movie stars—Forest Lawn, my fellow *KNOW* writers had nicknamed it—but compared to the other fossils eating in the Lounge that day, Skye was practically a teenager. She was officially forty-nine in Hollywood years, which meant she was closer to a girlish sixty. But she looked terrific. She still wore her hair in the same shaggy style, although now she kept her bangs from falling into her eyes by sashing it like a curtain to the side of her head with a ruby-and-diamond-studded bobby pin. I couldn't help myself; I sort of found her sexy. Even if the penis was, admittedly, a turnoff.

I broke the ice with an old magazine interview chestnut—the corny empty-your-purse-so-I-can-describe-its-contents shtick. Skye giggled and good-naturedly spilled her car keys, wallet, and checkbook onto the table. Then I buttered her up by referring to her early work—like the schlocky biker flick *Pussycat Has a Gun!*—as "neo-classics." She giggled again. Finally, I tiptoed toward the subject of her genitalia. "It must be difficult being famous," I said in my most sympathetic interviewer voice. "I mean, how do you deal with the gossip? Over the years you must have encountered at least one outrageous lie you've always wanted to correct. Tell me, what's the most outlandish thing you've ever heard about yourself?"

Skye wrinkled her forehead and thought for a moment, then gave up. "I never hear any gossip about myself," she said, giggling. "Not a word. But I'd love to know what people are saying. If you've heard of something, tell me. Honestly, I'd love to hear."

"Well," I said, "there's the rumor about the circumstances of your birth . . ."

"Really?" she said.

I was beginning to suspect that the hermaphrodite story wasn't 100 percent true, but it was too late to turn back. The penis had left the station. "You know," I finally blurted it out, "the rumor about you being born with male sex organs?"

The interview was over. Skye stuffed her car keys, wallet, and checkbook back into her purse and got up from the table. "I'm so sorry I asked you that question," I said, totally sincere. I made a mental note to shove that Monrovian snow globe up Carla's nose when I got back to New York. Skye gave me an icy stare. She was no longer giggling. "I'm sorry you asked that question, too," she replied. Then she dumped my chopped chef salad into my lap and left the restaurant.

So it took some time, but eventually I got the hang of the job. I learned the basic rules of talking to celebrities. How to save the toughest questions for last, so that if the star storms off the way Sissy Skye had I'd still have enough material in my tape recorder to write a story (I ended up getting only a half page for that interview). I learned to win over stars with flattery, no matter how painfully insincere ("I loved you in *Timecop*!") but also never to treat famous people like famous people—nobody likes a suck-up.

After a while, I got so comfortable interviewing stars I began to think of myself as a celebrity whisperer. Truth was, though, in my own way, I was growing more and more starstruck. I was collecting celebrities like prizes. After every interview, I would mentally hang a star's pelt in a trophy room in my brain, another specimen captured. I even invented a home version of the game that I would play when watching TV. Any time a celebrity I had interviewed popped up on the screen, I'd give myself points. Two if I'd talked to them on the phone, five if I'd interviewed them in person, and ten if I'd had sex with them. This last category was entirely theoretical, of course. Although one night I did rack up a record score when I happened to flip on *Entertainment Tonight* and caught a glimpse of Samantha and Johnny Mars on the red carpet at a premiere. I gave myself fifty points and declared myself a loser.

After that miserable parting of ways at the *KNOW* party, Samantha and I became "pals." She wouldn't have it any other way. She sent letters. She left messages. She mailed more letters (Sam was the last of the great letter writers; even while we were living together, she'd sometimes send me cards and notes). We were going to be friends whether

I liked it or not. And, whether I liked it or not, nothing more.

Needless to say, I didn't like it. I shook my fist at the heavens and cursed the name Johnny Mars. How dare this guy who had everything take the one thing from my life that mattered to me? I fantasized about throwing *him* out of an airplane and delivering my own devastating bon mot: "Get your own girlfriend, douchebag." But Samantha had been the biggest part of my life for as far back as I could remember, and I didn't know, didn't want to know, how to have a life without her. Besides, I figured my best chance of winning her back was to stick around, even if it meant masquerading as her buddy. When things went south with Mars—as I was pretty sure they would, eventually—I'd be there to help her pick up the pieces. I just needed to be patient.

In fact, there was a moment early on when I thought I might have an opening. One night, about a year after she moved into Johnny's penthouse, Samantha turned up at two in the morning at my new apartment, a bigger one-bedroom on a more civilized block in the West Village. As attached as I'd been to our old studio, it was haunted by Sammy's ghost. I was always stumbling on stray hairclips in the back of the closet or old bottles of her conditioner in a cupboard. I couldn't wait to get out. The best part of the move, though, was that I could finally buy a real bed and throw away that infernal sofa sleeper. There's nothing more awkward than having to pause in the middle of a date to wrestle with a spring-loaded mattress that's stuck halfway out of the couch.

"Can I come up?" Sammy asked through the intercom.

I could tell even through the static that she'd been crying. I pressed the button to let her into the building, then
remembered I wasn't alone. There was a naked girl sleeping in my new bed. This was a fairly common state of
affairs at the time. That's not meant as bragging. Part of
it, frankly, was biology, plain and simple—I was a guy in
my twenties. But I was also looking for validation. After
getting my heart pulverized by Samantha, I needed proof
that I was still lovable. Or at least attractive. I needed to
know that if Sammy didn't want me, a lot of other girls
did. So I slept with as many of them as I could, and that
turned out to be quite a few. "Where are you going?" the
girl in my bed—Cecilia, Cybille, Cintra, she had some
sort of exotic C-name—mumbled into the pillow as I
slipped into jeans and pulled on a sweater. "Nowhere," I
whispered back, inching toward the door. "I'm not going
anywhere."

"Oh, God, you're with somebody," Samantha said,
quickly turning back toward the elevator. "I'm so sorry—
I shouldn't have come." I grabbed her sleeve and insisted
she stay. Even in distress, she looked terrific. There was
no denying Sammy had acquired a polished new sheen
since she started dating a movie star. She dressed better,
or at least more expensively. Her nails were perfectly
manicured, something she never bothered with when
we were living together. And on this particular night, I
couldn't help notice, there was something almost incan-
descent about her skin. It was going to be tougher than
usual to pretend I wasn't still in love with her.

We sat out in the hallway and talked in whispers for
an hour. Sam and Johnny had had a fight earlier in the

evening. It was about the usual dumb stuff couples argue over, as well as the unusual stuff that couples fight about only if one of them happens to be an internationally famous superstar. "We check into a hotel and the mayor of the city and dozens of other people are there to greet him," Samantha explained. "And he just leaves me sitting in the car. It's like he forgets I'm there. It'd be funny," she went on, "but I have to admit it hurts." Samantha had other complaints, as well—about how women were constantly throwing themselves at Mars, even when she was standing right next to him—but as upsetting as all this was to her, I kept thinking that it didn't add up to her turning up at my door at two in the morning. I had the sense that there was something more going on with Sammy, something she wasn't saying.

I did my best to appear understanding and sympathetic, but in my head wheels were spinning within wheels. When Samantha found herself in trouble—whatever sort of trouble it was—whom had she turned to? She turned to me! That must mean something. I started wondering if this was the point in the script when Sammy realized that she didn't want to be with a movie star—she wanted to be with the boy next door. Finally, she was coming to her senses. She was understanding that what we had—a connection forged in the primordial ooze of our childhoods, a bond locking us together on a molecular level—was far more powerful than any fly-by-night romance with a Hollywood slickster. "So," I said, after we talked for a while, "are you really in love with this guy? I mean, truly, deeply in love? Are you sure?" What I was actually asking, of course, was whether she loved me instead.

Before Samantha could answer, the door to my apartment flew open and Cecilia-Cybille-Cintra, fully dressed and obviously annoyed, stormed into the hallway. "Asshole," she muttered under her breath as she stepped into the elevator. Sammy looked mortified, but after seeing that I didn't care, couldn't help cracking up. "I'm so sorry," she said after the elevator doors slid closed. "I spoiled your evening. And she looked so pretty." We talked a little while longer, then she said she had to go. She slipped into her coat and gave me a long hug. "Thanks for cheering me up," she said, kissing me softly on my nose. "You're a good friend." A month later, I read in the tabloids that Samantha and Johnny were married.

They'd been wed in a private ceremony—"exclusive," was the word the *Post* used—held at the star's 150-acre vacation ranch in Wyoming. Above the story was the single wedding photograph the newlyweds had released to the press, a shot of the happy couple beaming for the camera, in tuxedo and white gown, atop one of Mars's horses. I stared at the picture until my eyes bled.

5

I tried to fall in love again. Really, I did. I sure dated a lot. Although maybe "dates" isn't quite the right word for what I went on. They were more like drive-by fondlings. Or random acts of groping. Few of these "romances" had a life span longer than, say, a Jenny McCarthy sitcom.

It's not that I was such an amazing pickup artist. I was never the kind of smoothie who could reel a girl in from five barstools away with a slick line and a wink. On the contrary—I'd had the same girlfriend since I was twelve; I didn't have a clue how to pick up chicks. But I had a cool job with a regular paycheck, was not hideously disfigured, and was straight. In New York during the Great Man Shortage of the 1990s, that made me a catch.

Still, no matter who I went out with, I would always panic. I would wake up in the middle of the night next to a woman I barely knew and suddenly the walls would begin closing in. I'd stagger to the window, gasping for air. It was like claustrophobia, or gamophobia, or coulrophobia (or is that fear of clowns?). Whatever phobia I was suffering from, it made me feel as if the girl in my bed, whoever she was, had been the worst decision I'd ever made. It made me feel as if I'd stepped into a bear trap, and that I would need to chew off a limb to get free. To make matters worse, I was terrible at breaking up, no matter how much practice I got. To do it properly takes spadework. You have to seed the ground with subtle hints of dissatisfaction—calling off dinners at the last minute, sulking for no good reason—so that it's not too much of a shock when you drop the ax. There were times, I confess, when I took the easy way out and simply stopped answering my phone. "You're an asshole," one of my dates succinctly scrawled on a postcard she mailed from across town. She had a point.

In my defense, I did occasionally break the pattern. Every once in a while, I managed to keep a relationship going for whole weeks at a stretch. Sometimes even for a couple of months.

Darcy and I got into a fight on our very first date. We were at my apartment, in bed, and we started arguing about Cuba. I have no idea how the subject came up, but suddenly we were debating whether Castro had been good or bad for the Cuban people. I consider myself a card-carrying member of the liberal media conspiracy, but fiery, dark-eyed Darcy was an old-fashioned red-diaper baby from a famous family of wealthy American communists. Her great-grandfather had been one of the Hollywood Ten. Compared to her, I was a goose-stepping Nazi.

"Look at the literacy rate in Cuba!" she shouted, pulling the sheet up over her chest. "It's ninety-eight percent!"

"Terrific!" I shouted back, covering my privates with a

pillow. "Too bad there's nothing to read. There's no free press!"

We kept this up for months. We would fight, break up over some stupid argument, and then get back together again for a couple of weeks. For me, the comforting knowledge that a split was always imminent was the key to making the arrangement work. For Darcy, it must have been maddening. After we broke up for the last time, I heard she joined the Peace Corps and moved to China. If I could have gotten that far away from myself, I would have.

After Darcy, I met a bubbly blond stage actress at a bar in SoHo. As we sipped dirty martinis, Mindy told me about her role in an off-Broadway play that required partial nudity. To demonstrate how comfortable she was with the part, she lifted up her shirt, right in the middle of the bar, and revealed her flawless breasts. We went out for about six weeks. I never used the word "girlfriend" and never permitted her to call me "boyfriend," insisting on a rigid no-strings policy. It wasn't that monogamy bothered me—I didn't cheat on Mindy—it's just that after Sammy, the only way I could sustain even a short-term relationship was by pretending I wasn't in one. Mindy was a good enough actress to play the role for a while, but eventually she got bored and moved on to more interesting parts. She's now married to a hugely successful hedge-fund manager.

Jen was a knockout fashion stylist who happened to be the girlfriend of a semifamous TV actor—Derek Meecham, the guy who played Joey's dumber brother for a half season of *Friends*. I met her at a magazine photo shoot in TriBeCa and we instantly hit it off. Luckily for me, she'd been feeling ignored by her semifamous boyfriend and was having doubts about their relationship. As far as I was concerned, the fact that she had a semifamous boyfriend only made her more attractive. Here was my chance to do to a celebrity what a celebrity had done to me. Even if he wasn't really a celebrity. After about a month of secret dating, though, I discovered that I really liked Jen. She was sweet and vulnerable, but with a wicked sense of humor and a dead-sexy way of telling dirty jokes. Then, one night as we lay in bed, she made a deal-breaking mistake. She suggested she break it off with the semifamous boyfriend. "So we can be closer," she explained, cuddling. "So we can be together, for real."

I nodded but didn't say anything. I was too busy studying Jen's ankles. I hadn't noticed it until just then, but they were starting to look thick.

One of the things making it especially hard for me to fall for another woman was the fact that Samantha seemed to be everywhere I turned. Within a few months of moving in with Johnny Mars, she was suddenly popping up all over TV. I'd be lounging at home in my boxer shorts, flipping channels, and—bang!—there she'd be in a laundry detergent commercial playing a pretty young mom in an apron. I'd try to watch *Melrose Place* and—boom!—there'd she be in the background, an extra at Shooters Bar. One night I spotted her on a slab in an episode of *Law & Order*. Even as a corpse, she made my heart go pitter-patter. I was glad her career was going so well, but this was getting ridiculous.

Samantha wasn't turning up at my doorstep at two in the morning anymore. But after she got married she did develop a weird habit of calling me at odd hours, usually from distant lands in far-flung time zones. Once she woke me in the middle of the night with a call from Paris, where Mars was accepting an honorary degree from the Sorbonne.

"Jessica Rabbit or the Little Mermaid?" she began the conversation without bothering with a hello.

"What?"

"*Jessica Rabbit or the Little Mermaid?*" she repeated more emphatically.

It took my brain a second or two to spin up out of sleep mode and recognize what Sammy was doing. She was playing the game where we'd take turns choosing which pop culture character we'd rather make out with. "Jessica Rabbit," I answered. "No, wait, what are the biological implications of having a tail?" We used to play all the time back when we were kids. Ginger or Mary Ann? Wilma or Betty? For her, Mike Seaver or Alex P. Keaton? Brandon or Dylan? It had been a while and I was out of practice. "Um," I said, returning the volley, "Ren or Stimpy?"

There was no reason for the call. Every once in a while, Samantha just needed a reminder that I was there, still floating in high orbit around her life. I didn't mind. Even in the middle of the night—*especially* in the middle of the night—I found the sound of her voice soothing.

I saw Samantha in the flesh once in a while, too. Every six months or so we would get together for dinner or drinks in what became, for me, an excruciating exercise in superhuman restraint. I would have to pretend not to sniff her hair when she squeezed past me into her chair at the restaurant. I'd have to try to ignore how soft and inviting her lips looked when I watched her nibble on a piece of lettuce. There was a strict choreography to these dinners. We'd begin by talking about Johnny. How great he was. The amusing comments and brilliant observations and amazing career moves he'd made recently. Then we'd chat about Sammy for a bit, and how great she was, until we moved on to how great I was. But for all the cheery bravado, I wasn't sure Sammy was doing so terrific. I knew for a fact that I wasn't.

Being a movie star's wife had obvious advantages. Money. Status. Even a certain degree of spousal-reflected fame. Sammy didn't get asked for her autograph, but her new last name definitely elevated her status. She always arrived at our dinners in a chauffeur-driven town car, sometimes even a full-blown limo, and we never had to wait to be seated. Even at the most crowded restaurants, even when we didn't have reservations, right away we'd be escorted to the best table in the house. But there was a downside, too. So long as she was married to Johnny, Sammy would always be a supporting player in her own life. She'd always get second billing to her husband. No matter what else she did, no matter what she accomplished, it could never compete with being a superstar's wife.

What's more, Sammy had to share her husband with the entire world. That wasn't always a whole lot of fun. Once, at one of our dinners, Sammy told me about a trip she had taken with Johnny to Tokyo. They were met at the airport by hundreds of hysterical fans (apparently, Jack Montana was big in Japan). The mob was so excited by

his arrival that the Tokyo police had to swarm in and res-
cue Mars, but not before a Japanese schoolgirl got close
enough to rip a sleeve from Johnny's shirt. The police
quickly hustled him through a security door and gave him
a motorcade escort to his hotel. It was an hour before anybody realized that Sammy was still at the airport with the
luggage. Samantha laughed when she told the story, but it
still sounded pretty humiliating.

Mercifully, Samantha never suggested bringing her
husband to one of our dinners. I no longer had the slightest desire to meet Johnny Mars. I'd rather have spent an
evening trapped in an elevator with Sissy Skye and her
gynecologist-urologist. The closest I'd come to him so
far was when I returned one of Sammy's calls and made
the mistake of dialing her home number. Johnny picked
up. "Oh, so you're Max, eh?" he rumbled into the phone.
"I've heard a lot about you." I tried to speak but the
words caught in my throat. "Um, I've heard a lot about
you, too," I finally stuttered back. After that, I made it a
point never to call Sammy at home.

But I did come perilously close to an in-person
encounter with Special Agent Jack Montana in the spring
of 2008, about two years into their marriage. The near
miss occurred at the Magistrate Theater on Forty-second
Street, at the New York premiere of the Kenneth Branagh–
Julia Ormond fourteenth-century romance *Canterbury's
Pilgrim.*

As a writer for *KNOW,* I got invited to lots of movie premieres. I loved attending them. The roving klieg lights.

The shouting paparazzi. The thrill of strolling down a red carpet. It gave me tingles. Best of all, though, if you brought a date to a movie opening you were all but guaranteed to get lucky later. At that time, I was trying to get lucky with Lacy, a super-cute Pilates instructor with delusions of modeling. It was only our second date, but from the way Lacy held my hand during the cab ride to the theater, I was feeling optimistic. Especially since she had told me during our first date that she was a big Kenneth Branagh fan. When we got to the entrance and she saw Branagh himself, in the flesh, glad-handing fans and signing autographs, Lacy let out a delighted squeal.

Then I nearly let out a squeal. I saw another celebrity on the rope line, a hulking, towering figure who was whipping up the crowd even more than Branagh. It was Johnny Mars. Samantha was trailing a few yards behind him on the red carpet, flanked by Johnny's publicist and agent, a grim smile pasted on her face.

"Um, hold up a sec," I told Lacy. "We can't go in yet."

Lacy gave me a look like I'd strangled her favorite kitten, but I was frozen on the pavement. Why hadn't I anticipated this possibility? Mars and Samantha didn't attend many premieres (the really big stars seldom do, unless the movie is their own) but this was exactly the sort of pseudo-highbrow fare—a Miramax period piece about Geoffrey Chaucer's love life—that would appeal to the action star's intellectual pretensions. How could I have been so stupid? But there he was, along with his beautiful wife, drawing more cheers than any of the *Canterbury's Pilgrim*'s stars. In fact, Branagh and Ormond looked a little pissed off. Lacy, naturally, was thrilled by all the excitement, but I was mortified. I'd seen enough science fiction movies to know what happened when matter was introduced to antimatter. If I met Johnny Mars it would mean the end of the universe. Or, at the very least, an incredibly awkward handshake.

What was I supposed to do? Walk up to Samantha and say hello? At a public event like a premiere, that wouldn't be so easy. Before I got anywhere near Sammy, Mars's bodyguards would have me in a headlock, while I flailed around trying to get Samantha's attention. Pathetic. And say I did slip past the guards to say hi—or say Sammy just happened to catch sight of me in the crowd—that would be just as bad. Samantha would feel obligated to introduce me to her husband. I'd feel obligated to introduce Mars and her to Lacy, who was now pulling at my arm with all her muscle. "C'mon!" she moaned. "What's the matter with you! Everybody is going into the theater!"

We managed to get to our balcony seats without being spotted. Lacy was a little annoyed by my behavior outside the theater, but she let it go. As the curtains parted on the screen, she reached across the armrest to give my hand a forgiving squeeze. I didn't watch the film. Instead, as young Chaucer scribbled in his garret during the opening sequence, I scanned the theater looking for Johnny Mars's enormous head. It wasn't hard to spot—it towered like a giraffe's over everybody else's in the VIP section. I spent the next hour drilling holes with my eyes into the back of his skull.

Mars was one of those stars, like Robert De Niro and Adam Sandler, who never gave interviews. But a lot was written about him anyway. I know, because after he stole my girlfriend, I read everything. Just to torture myself. He had a classic action star origin tale. He was born in Alaska, the son of a lumberjack. Moved to Hollywood when he was twenty, where he found work on construction crews that helped build movie sets at the studios. One day while sawing two-by-fours on the Paramount lot, he got tapped on the shoulder by a casting director. Next thing he knows, he's got a nonspeaking role in *Cyborg Prophecies,* playing a mute robot. Over the next ten years, the roles got progressively bigger (he played a speaking robot in *Cyborg Prophecies 2,* and a hockey star turned prison inmate in *Penalty Box*), until his big break came at thirty, when he got cast as hard-drinking, hard-driving, hard-quipping FBI agent Jack Montana, the role that shot him to the very top of the action A-list. He'd been playing the part, off and on, for more than fifteen years.

The funny thing about Mars, however, was that even though he commanded the adoration of the masses, even though he was a millionaire many times over, even though he could have any woman he wanted (including the only one *I* wanted), he wasn't satisfied. The ranch in Wyoming, the penthouse on the Upper West Side, the private jets and personal chefs and chauffeur-driven limos—it wasn't enough. More than all of that, more than anything else, he wanted to be taken seriously.

Ironically, the same things that helped make him an action star—the soaring height, the huge muscular build, the growling voice so rumbling it could set off car alarms—also made him a difficult fit for more serious parts. He was actually a pretty decent actor, but who's going to buy a six-foot-three, 245-pound Willy Loman? Still, Mars refused to give up. He was always throwing himself into roles he had no business playing. Macbeth, Ishmael, Jean Valjean. I hated his guts, but there was still a smidgen of fan left inside me. I couldn't help but grudgingly admire his tenacity. He was determined to prove his acting chops, even though all anybody really wanted to watch him do was push bad guys off monuments and out of airplanes and make jokes about the first step being a doozy.

When I finally pulled my eyes from the back of Mars's head, Julia Ormond was up on the screen in a suit of armor, kissing Kenneth Branagh. I had no idea why. I hadn't been following the plot. I looked over at Lacy, who was smiling in a daze, a Twizzler dangling from her mouth. She was clearly entranced by the film. Then I looked for the nearest exit.

"Lacy," I whispered in her ear. No response. "Lacy," I repeated a little louder.

"Mmm?" she answered.

"I have to go." It was true. I couldn't stand another minute of looking at Johnny Mars in his VIP seat, his big beefy arm wrapped around my dainty Samantha's shoulders. But Lacy gave me a look like she'd caught me molesting that kitten I had strangled earlier.

"What?" she asked, her voice rising in anger. "Are you nuts!" The couple in the row in front of us turned around and glared. "What about the party afterward?" Lacy went on, ignoring the commotion we were starting to cause. "You have to take me to the premiere party! I want to meet Kenneth Branagh!"

"You can still go," I whispered, reaching into my breast pocket for the party tickets and stuffing them into her lap.

"You can still have fun. I just can't be here right now. I'm really sorry."

"Oh, no!" Lacy all but shouted. "I'm not going to the party by myself. You have to go with me! We're on a date!"

People all around the balcony were starting to shush us. I'd never been shushed in a theater before and didn't know what to do. So I started shushing, too. Big mistake. "YOU'RE SHUSHING ME?!" Lacy yelled into my face, so loudly that people in the orchestra section began turning around to glower. "*YOU* DON'T SHUSH *ME!*" A few more seconds of this and we'd draw the attention of the entire theater, including Mars and Samantha. I did the only thing I could. I hid my face in my jacket lapels, climbed over Lacy's seat, and dashed as quickly as I could out of the theater. The last thing I heard was Lacy yelling after me. "ASSHOLE!"

Once again, I had to concede this point.

6

As a member of the Hollywood press, I saw fame from the outside looking in. I was a Talmudic scholar of pop culture, but never part of the biblical text. On one occasion, though, I did get a tiny taste of what life was like inside the fishbowl. In the fall of 1999, my picture was in *KNOW* magazine. Not even my father recognized me— my face was covered in fur and I was wearing large prosthetic rodent ears—but I was in *KNOW* all the same, just like a real celebrity.

This was for a story on a sci-fi TV show called *Dark Matter,* about a microscopic alternate universe that existed in subatomic space. The concept was based almost entirely on the classic stoner epiphanot in *Animal House*— "Okay, so that means our whole solar system could be, like, one tiny atom in the fingernail of some other giant being . . ."—but the series became an instant cult hit. So my editors arranged for me to appear in one of its episodes as an alien extra—a sort of human-hamster hybrid—then write about the experience for the magazine.

I arrived at the Paramount lot at six in the morning and spent three hours in a makeup chair being turned into a "VIP alien," as my hamsteroid character was described in the call sheet. I learned that I'd be making my TV debut as part of a crowd of aliens waiting in line at Passport and Immigration Control at an interdimensional space-port—a long panoramic shot of assorted otherworldly travelers getting their space luggage checked and their space documents stamped by customs officer robots. But when I stepped onto the soundstage and saw the other extraterrestrials, I felt a pang of alien envy. They had much cooler makeup than I did. One guy looked like a Rastafar-ian orangutan; another like the love spawn of Jabba the Hutt and Mrs. Potato Head. All I did during my seven seconds on film was stand next to a scantily clad reptile woman with four breasts and pretend to make small talk. "Whadya expect?" the lizard lady asked me between takes. "That we'd do scenes from *Hedda Gabler*?"

When the article came out, the same week my episode aired, I stopped at newsstands all over New York to gaze upon my furry face. Within days I started getting letters from readers requesting autographed copies. I felt like an idiot writing my name on my picture with a Sharpie, but I answered every piece of mail, just like a real star (or a real star's assistant). It didn't take long for me to grow a star-size ego, as well. When I scrutinized my face in *KNOW*, I started to notice a tiny red vein in my left eye—a flaw that would have been airbrushed away had I been a real celebrity. I cursed myself for not demanding photo approval.

A few weeks later, as I was waiting in line at a video

store, I experienced another drawback to fame. Let's just say I was doing research for that big exposé on the adult movie industry I'd been planning to get around to writing. When it was my turn at the register, I removed the video from under my arm and discreetly slid it—my renter's ID card covering the naughty bits—to the skinny, bespectacled nerd behind the counter. He read my name, looked at my face, read my name again, then looked at my face. "You're the guy who wrote about *Dark Matter* in *KNOW* magazine!" he informed the whole store. "You're the guy who got to be an alien!" I smiled grimly and nudged the video closer to the kid, hoping he'd put it in a bag already. "This is so cool!" he said, picking up the box and waving it around. "I can't believe you're renting a video in my store!"

Finally, I experienced the final stage of the celebrity life cycle, fame's death throcs. I turned on a new episode of *Dark Matter* and saw that my hamster was being played by another actor. In fact, he'd been given lines to speak! To think, I developed that character, I brought it to life, and now some upstart in rodent ears was taking over just as the part was getting interesting. I knew exactly how Bette Davis felt at the end of *All About Eve*.

I may not have been a real celebrity, but I got to live like one, especially when traveling on assignment. At the end of the 1990s, before terrorism and stock market crashes erased the last vestiges of glamour from jet travel, there was a luxury service between New York and Los Angeles called Imperial Airways. It operated the most pimped-out commercial fleet in the sky. The front end of its lavishly configured DC-8s and 727s had private berths, like on a train, so that first-class passengers could slide shut a frosted-glass door and cross the country in privacy. Even Imperial's "coach" section, where I usually sat, had cushy oversize red-leather swivel-loungers, provided linen and crystal dinner service, and was always packed with celebs. It was like the Golden Globes at thirty thousand feet. I loved it.

I became a frequent flyer on Imperial, shuttling between the coasts once or twice a month for interviews. When I landed in LA, I would always rent a zippy convertible and stay at the posh Four Seasons Hotel, the pale pink palace on the east edge of Beverly Hills that was the red-hot center of Hollywood's mediaverse. This was where the studios put up talent from out of town, where many of the film industry's junkets were held, and where you could always catch a glimpse of a celebrity in a swimsuit at the pool. The Four Seasons had a frequent-stayer bonus: After forty visits, they gave you a terrycloth bathrobe, the fluffiest on Earth, with your initials monogrammed on it. I had two of them. During a brief hipster stage, I grew a goatee and switched to the grittier Chateau Marmont on Sunset, where you could always catch a glimpse of a celebrity overdosing at the pool. But eventually I shaved and returned to my fortress on Doheny. The Four Seasons felt more like home to me than home. I don't know how it was that I didn't see any problem with that.

When I first started spending time in LA, I made the mistake of comparing the city's geo-demographics to Manhattan's. Beverly Hills was the Upper East Side with palm trees. Venice was the East Village with sand. West

Hollywood was Chelsea with actual, atmospherically created rainbows. After a while, though, I began to see that the true comparison wasn't with New York City, but with Westchester. Being in Los Angeles, I realized, was a lot like being sixteen years old in the suburbs when my dad went away on a business trip and left me home alone with the keys to his Cadillac and a cookie jar filled with "emergency" cash. LA is a city filled with grown-up children spending money they shouldn't be spending and driving cars they shouldn't be driving. It's a town without any adult supervision.

It is also a city filled with beautiful women who dress like porn stars even when picking up a carton of organic orange juice at the grocery store (the men, meanwhile, dress like little boys, in short pants and T-shirts). I thought LA might be a solution to my commitment phobia problem. I was traveling there twice a month but seldom staying longer than two or three days, the time it took to turn around an interview or a set visit. Theoretically, that was also just long enough for a brief romantic encounter. Sadly, though, my plan to make LA my sexual playground didn't pan out. California-style dating was too alien to me. I never did get the hang of it. In New York, if you met a girl at a party, you might ask her where she went to school or what she had majored in. In Los Angeles, you asked where she was repped and who did her head shots. In New York, when you invited a girl on a date, it was assumed you'd meet at the restaurant. In LA, transport to and from dinner was a complex minuet. Did you pick her up? Or was that presumptuous? Either way, what you drove was critical. In Hollywood, there is no more important status marker than the make and model of your car. I once picked up an LA woman for a date in a brand-new high-performance BMW M3—the rental place had upgraded me from my usual Mustang—and I knew right away I'd be getting lucky. "Wow!" my date said, slowly running a finger along a door panel. "I've never gone out with a car this nice before."

My real personal life may have been a wasteland, but my relationships with the stars were improving. I began to see myself less as a celebrity whisperer and more as an anthropologist, the Jane Goodall of fame, hacking my way through the Hollywood jungle in order to study the mysterious primates who lived in this strange Serengeti with valet parking. I once flew to LA just to spend an afternoon hovering in a helicopter over the Academy Awards for an aerial photo spread that would give *KNOW* readers a bald-spot-view of the stars. At eight hundred feet, with a photographer dangling out the window in a safety harness, it felt exactly like we were filming a Discovery Channel nature documentary. As a species, *Homo sapiens* are drawn toward fame like leopards to gazelles—and I wanted to know how come. When you think about it, the concept of celebrity is relatively new to human society. Yet clearly it triggers primal impulses in us all. What itch in our monkey brains are we scratching when we turn and stare at Val Kilmer in an airport? What ancient Darwinian impulse are we satisfying when we ask Reese Witherspoon for her autograph?

At the start of the twenty-first century, the whole world

seemed to be going celebrity crazy. New celeb-focused magazines were popping up on newsstands every week, while otherwise serious newspapers, like *The New York Times,* began publishing box office tallies as if they were sports scores. When Tom Cruise and Nicole Kidman announced their divorce, the networks interrupted regular TV programming to broadcast the news as though it were the moon landing. *KNOW* magazine had been bitten by the celebrity bug, as well, and was putting more movie stars on its covers than ever. That was great for me—I got to write a lot of those celebrity stories. I still felt driven to understand the shimmering world that had stolen Sammy from me. I still saw fame as a mystery that needed solving.

So I expanded my research. I talked to a real anthropologist—a woman who spent years in an actual jungle studying monkeys—about celebrity and why it mattered to us humans. Her theory was that fame was a throwback to the primate need for an alpha male. "In the ape world, the alpha male eats whatever he wants to and sleeps with whoever he wants to," she explained while I tried not to envision Johnny Mars as a giant monkey swinging in to take my Sammy away from me. "The only difference is that the ape doesn't get a limousine." I talked to a psychologist about the phenomenon, and his take was that fame was a sort of mental illness—acquired situational narcissism, he called the affliction. Another expert in media sociology saw fame as a "drug" that had hooked the whole planet. "We've all become addicts," he said, sounding strung out. "There have been studies. People experience withdrawal symptoms if they don't get their dose of Brad and Jen or Justin and Britney."

You'd think the best people to ask about fame would be famous people, but you'd be disappointed. Whenever I interviewed a big star, I snuck in a question about the nature of fame and a celebrity's place in the universe. I'd usually get blank stares and cricket noises. Some stars pretended to hate fame, even though it was obvious they secretly loved it. A few pretended to love it, even though it was obvious they secretly hated it. But not a lot of celebrities seemed to give fame much serious, philosophical thought. Even the smartest celebs—the ones who put on horn-rimmed glasses and discussed Chechnya on *Charlie Rose*—seemed bored by the subject. To them, it was like the weather. Some days it was nice being famous, other days it was crappy. Either way, they were powerless over it, and therefore not all that interested in it.

Every once in a while, though, I'd run into a star who surprised me.

"Here's the thing about fame," Alistair Lyon offered as he did a lazy backstroke across the deep end of his kidney-shaped pool. I was kneeling at the edge, holding my microrecorder over the sparkling water, hoping Lyon's splashing sounds weren't going to be the only part of the interview I'd be able to hear on the tape. "It doesn't end world hunger. It doesn't cure cancer. Fame doesn't even cure loneliness. It doesn't make you stronger or protect you from harm or give you any superpowers. It's just perfume. That's all it is. It makes you smell nice. It's the world's greatest deodorant."

Lyon had gained a lot of weight since winning his fourth Academy Award the year before, for playing Adolf Hitler in *The Bunker,* a big-screen remake of the

1981 TV movie that earned Anthony Hopkins an Emmy. He was so huge, the waterline actually dipped a notch when he finally hauled himself out of the pool. The fattening up was all part of the fifty-nine-year-old Aussie superstar's preparation for his next role—he'd be playing Winston Churchill in Ron Howard's adaptation of William Manchester's *The Last Lion*. No actor in the last thirty years had brought to life so many great historical figures. Abraham Lincoln, Albert Einstein, Attila the Hun, Francis Bacon, Lyndon Johnson, Julius Caesar, Yuri Gagarin, Buffalo Bill, Babe Ruth, Benjamin Disraeli, Leonardo da Vinci, Ernest Hemingway—if he was famous and dead, chances are Lyon had won a statuette for playing him.

I loved interviewing stars in their homes—you learn so much about celebrities from their tchotchkes. Lyon's mid-century glass-and-stone mansion in the Hollywood Hills was filled with Eames chairs and Nelson benches and Knoll tables. A vast wraparound balcony off the sunken living room offered a breathtaking panoramic view of the city. Hanging on the walls were more Picassos and Pollocks and Warhols than at the Getty. If Lyon weren't such a world-famous ladies man, I'd swear he was gay—his taste in home decor was *that* good. Attractive young German-accented Aryans of both genders—Lyon must have picked them up while playing Hitler—were fluttering all over, answering phone calls, mixing pitchers of mimosas, and rushing plates of caviar omelets and other snacks from the kitchen to the pool. The overhead costs of being Alistair Lyon had to be staggering. Luckily, he was rich.

"The trick to living with fame," Lyon went on as an assistant wrapped his dripping wet body in a towel as big as a mainsail, "is not to take it too seriously. You shouldn't cling to it. You shouldn't try to hold fame in your grip. Fame is like money—you're just borrowing it. Someday you're going to die, and somebody else is going to get it." Another assistant arrived with a platter of freshly rolled sushi. Lyon sniffed a piece before popping it into his mouth. "Do you want to be famous, young man?" he asked, giving me a curious stare. "Is that your dream? Is that why you have so many questions about it?"

No celebrity had ever asked me that before—interviews were always one-way conversations. I asked, they answered. But now that a star finally had asked me a serious question, I found myself stumbling for an answer. Of course, like every journalist, I'd wondered what life on the other side of the tape recorder might be like. Maybe I was even a little jealous. The actor stuffing his face with sushi in front of me had an earned annual income larger than several European nations. He had a watch on his wrist worth more than most people's houses. He had a shelf in his living room cluttered with little golden men. What exactly did I have? Still, fame wasn't something I had ever even remotely craved. I honestly never hungered for the spotlight or fantasized about signing autographs. No, my fascination with celebrity was driven by a totally different sort of ego deficiency.

"I just want the money and adoration," I answered Lyon, half-joking. "I don't care about the rest."

In fact, all I really wanted was the girl.

7

"I'm on a beach in Mykonos," Sammy said. "That's in Greece, in case you didn't know. And I'm not wearing a top."

It was three in the morning in New York—ten in the morning on the clothing-optional Greek beach Sammy was calling me from on her cell—and I had been floating in deep dream space when the phone woke me up. As accustomed as I was to her late-night calls, it always took me a few seconds to rev my brain up to conversational speed. I leaned back on my pillow and imagined Sammy strolling bare-chested on the shores of the sparkling Mediterranean, her naked skin shimmering in the sunshine, until I let a small groan escape into the phone. I covered it up with a fake cough. "What are you doing in Mykonos?" I groggily asked.

"Johnny is doing location scouting for the next Montana movie," she said. "They're thinking of shooting a scene at the Acropolis. They want Johnny to throw bad guys off a European monument in this movie. Something about it being good for overseas box office. Personally, I think it's a great idea. I love it here. The beaches are spectacular. Did I mention I'm not wearing a top?"

Sammy could be a terrible tease, but she didn't mean anything by it. We had known each other so well for so long, it was impossible for her to be anything other than completely herself. I, on the other hand, had no such luxury. I was still cloaking myself in platonic sheep's clothing, pretending to be fine with being just friends, while secretly hoping that her marriage to Johnny would fall apart. In the meantime, though, I had to be careful. If Sammy knew how I truly felt about her—what picturing her topless on a Greek beach did to my respiratory system—she might pull back. I couldn't risk that.

"I've never been to Greece," I said. "I should find a Greek movie set and get an assignment. Sounds like you're beautiful. *It's* beautiful. Greece, that is . . . being beautiful . . ."

"You know," she said, whispering into her cell phone, "the beaches here aren't just topless—they're bottomless, too. But I don't know if I could handle that. I can't really see myself being totally naked on a beach, can you?"

Oh, I could imagine it, all right. In fact, I had enough footage of Samantha stored in the film cans of my fantasy life to splice together an epic longer than *Shoah*. And not *all* of it was sex related. Sometimes, for instance, I'd fantasize about time travel. I'd flip the calendar back to the night in 1995 when Sammy turned up at my apartment at two in the morning after her fight with her new movie star boyfriend. In my rewrite, when I ask her if she truly loves Johnny, her big brown eyes fill with tears. "I'm still in love with you," she tells me. We embrace passionately. The next day, Page Six leads with a story about how Johnny Mars's girlfriend has dumped him for a dashing magazine writer in the West Village. The *Daily News* reports that Sammy is "swooning."

In another fantasy, I'd travel a little further back, to the day in 1994 when Sammy got the letter from the Concord Theater Festival. In the version in my head, though, she gets rejected and never goes to Massachusetts and never meets Johnny Mars. Instead, she sticks with me. Miraculously, I become a better boyfriend, more attentive, less selfish. I remember her birthdays, buy her the sorts of presents she likes, bring her flowers not just on Valentine's Day but every day. I stop taking her for granted. We get married at her parents' house, in the backyard, under the apple tree. Sammy's mom cries at the sight of her daughter in white, just like she did during Sam's performance in *Fiddler on the Roof* in high school.

"How are things with Johnny?" I asked, sitting up in bed, wishing I smoked cigarettes.

"Super great," Samantha said. I could hear the waves lapping the shore in the background. According to Sammy, Johnny was always "super great," but he never seemed to be around. "I haven't seen him in five days," she went on. "He dropped me off at this resort in Mykonos and then took off for Athens with some producers. I mean, how long does it take to look at a three-thousand-year-old Greek temple?"

"It's a pretty big temple," I offered. I couldn't tell her what I was really thinking—that Johnny was probably spending the five days in an Athenian hotel suite, danc-

ing like Zorba on a coffee table while half-naked Greek
groupies smashed plates around his feet. How come he
was always away whenever Sammy called? Or was it
that she called me only when he wasn't around? Either
way, I couldn't help but wonder if Johnny was faithful
to his wife. As a general rule, movie stars aren't exactly
renowned for monogamy.

"Oh, by the way," Sammy changed the subject, "I read
one of your articles on the plane out here. The interview
you did with the *Spider-Man* guy . . ."

"Tobey Maguire . . ."

"Yeah. It was great. I knew you were going to be a terrific writer one day, Max. Remember who pushed you into
journalism?"

"You did. It was part of your master plan for us, the
great writer/actress team. But, you know, I don't recall
anybody mentioning you marrying a movie star as part
of the deal."

"Yeah, well, sorry about that," Sammy said, laughing.
"But, you know, life happens, right? It's natural, isn't it?
You grow up, you meet new people . . ."

"You smash your boyfriend's heart into a thousand
pieces," I said, but not out loud. Sammy was right, of
course—it was only natural and normal to grow up and
leave your first love behind. Most people managed it without a hitch. But not me. If falling out of love with your
childhood sweetheart was a rite of passage into adulthood, I was still waiting to grow up.

"Besides," Sammy went on, "look how well it's all
worked out! You get to work for a fabulous magazine, I
get to run around with my top off on a nude Greek beach,

and we get to be best friends for the rest of our lives. That's not so bad, right? I mean, all things considered, that's pretty good, isn't it?"

"Yes," I said, biting my pillow. "It's super great."

When you're an unknown actress and you hook up with a movie star, you're going to take some lumps. Before Nicole Kidman won an Oscar, she was sneeringly referred to as "Mrs. Tom Cruise." Before Gwyneth Paltrow won hers, she was condescendingly known as Brad Pitt's plus one.

Samantha had a similar problem. Being Johnny Mars's wife opened lots of doors, but it raised just as many eyebrows. Every casting agent in New York would gladly meet with her, but not one took her seriously as an actress. Still, Samantha took herself seriously. Between traveling to Greece and other exotic lands with her husband, she kept plugging away at auditions. Eventually, she landed gigs. Playing a brainwashed CIA operative on an episode of *Alias,* for instance. Or a bus-wreck victim on an episode of *ER.* They were decent parts, with lines of dialogue and everything, a definite step up from portraying a dead body on a slab in *Law & Order.* But they weren't the sort of roles that were likely to springboard a career.

Then, in 2002, Sammy got one of the leads in a small indie drama called *Losers Weepers.* It was about two sisters in the 1950s who inherit and run a failing Italian restaurant in a small town on the Jersey Shore. One sister, played by Christina Ricci, is a hard-nosed realist who keeps the books; the other, Sammy's character, is an emotional chef who creates magnificent gourmet meals that none of the local rubes appreciate. When their longtime waiter quits to join a rival restaurant, the sisters place a help-wanted ad. Enter Marc Anthony, playing a dishy immigrant "guido" just off the boat from Rome. Both sisters end up falling in love with their new waiter and go to war with each other for his affections.

It was shot in just five weeks at a rented studio space in the Chelsea Piers for only $3 million, less than the moisturizer budget on one of Johnny's films. But it was the most charming, delightful little picture I'd seen in years. And Sammy—she was beyond enchanting. She must have trained like crazy for the role, because she handled a chef's knife like a juggler handles pins. In one scene, her character power-chops a bushel of carrots while having a screaming argument with her sister. The blade flashes so fast, it could almost qualify as a special effect. In another scene, Sammy's character is making bread with Marc Anthony's. She massages and kneads the dough so sensually, so carnally, the movie should have been rated NC-17.

I saw the film at its "premiere," which took place in a screening room in TriBeCa. There was no money in the budget for klieg lights or red carpets or any sort of festivities—just a table in the lobby with a tray of crusty Brie and a few bottles of warm chardonnay. I'd been dreading going, not because I didn't want to see the movie, or Samantha, but because I knew Johnny would be there. I'd managed to steer clear of the star since that near-miss at the *Canterbury's Pilgrim* debut four years earlier, but my luck was running out. This was his wife's big night. I would finally have to meet him. At least this time I hadn't brought a date.

But as I stood at the entrance holding flowers for Sam—something I never thought to do when we were still a couple—I didn't see Johnny in the crowd. And a meager crowd it was. Only about thirty people were milling about the lobby, mostly dressed in T-shirts and jeans. The only two stars in attendance were Sammy and Christina Ricci, who were in a corner chatting with some agent types. When Sam saw me enter, she smiled, waved, and made a beeline for me.

"I'm so glad you came!" she said, giving me a big hug before taking her roses. "I know it's not exactly Grauman's, but I wanted you here. I'm really proud of this movie. To tell you the truth, it's the first thing I've done I've actually wanted you to see."

"Where's Johnny?" I asked. I figured he was in the men's room or outside taking an important call. I was still bracing for the handshake I'd been putting off for years.

"Oh, Johnny couldn't be here," Sammy said, a little embarrassed. "He had to go to Cleveland for a meeting with one of the merchandisers. There's a problem with the new Jack Montana action figure—the head keeps popping off whenever you move the arms. Toys "R" Us is threatening to sue. But Johnny's already seen my movie. His production company helped finance it . . ."

"He's in Cleveland?" I repeated. I couldn't believe my luck. Once again I'd managed to postpone the inevitable. Even better, I had upstaged my movie star rival. This was the biggest moment in Sammy's career, the opening of her very first film, and he couldn't bother to be here for it. Sammy had never missed one of Johnny's premieres. She was arm candy for her husband at countless show-biz events. But he went to Cleveland because he was more interested in his action figures. Actually, when I thought about it, Johnny and I had a lot in common. He was self-ish and self-involved, too. The difference, though, was that I had learned my lesson. I had wised up. I had shown up, with flowers. "I'm sorry to hear I missed him," I lied. "I was really looking forward to meeting him."

Losers Weepers ended up being released in eight the-aters, where it grossed a grand total of $225,000 and was never seen again. It didn't even make enough money to justify a video release. I tried to get *KNOW*'s film critic to see it—a rave review in the magazine could have made all the difference—but he couldn't have been less inter-ested. "I despise movies set in the 1950s," he told me after I explained the plot of *Losers Weepers.* "I find the era depressing."

"Really?" I pressed him. "*American Graffiti? Diner? Raging Bull?* You find those movies depressing? *The God-father?* You find that one depressing?" He wouldn't budge.

A couple of weeks later, after *Losers Weepers* ran its pathetic theatrical course, my phone rang at two in the morning. Naturally, it was Sammy. For once, she was placing a local call, from her and Johnny's penthouse uptown.

"I just wanted to tell you how much it meant to me

that you came to my movie," she said. "It was my party but you were pretty much my only friend there."

"I loved it. Honestly. I'm not just saying that," I told her. "You were fantastic. I still can't get over how you chopped those carrots. I had no idea you were so handy with a knife."

"Maybe I can get a job as a chef." She laughed. "'Cause I don't think I'm going to get many more as an actress."

"Oh, I don't know about that," I said. "You never can tell what's going to happen. This time next year, you could be as famous as Johnny."

8

Six months later, in the summer of 2003, I was in my office at *KNOW*'s New York headquarters opening packages of swag—the free T-shirts and baseball caps and bobble-heads the studios send to reporters to promote new releases—when Carla poked her head in my door. "You know Samantha Mars, right? You went to high school with her or something? Are you still in contact with her?"

"Yeah, I know her a little," I said. "Why? What's up?"

"You haven't heard? Turn on CNN. Johnny Mars has been in an accident."

I madly flipped through the channels on the TV in my office until I found Aaron Brown behind his desk. A picture of Johnny was boxed off in one corner of the screen. "The extent of his injuries is still unknown, but from what's been confirmed so far it sounds like it could be quite serious," the laconic CNN anchor was reporting. "We have a specialist on the phone with us now, Dr. Jordan Charles. Dr. Charles, what can you tell us about

what's happened to Johnny Mars? What can you specu-
late about his condition?"

I sat in front of my TV watching in stunned silence
as details of the accident slowly emerged. Johnny had
been in South Dakota shooting his eleventh Jack Montana movie, *Don't Tread on Me,* when a stunt went
horribly, horribly wrong. They were filming an action
sequence on Mount Rushmore that involved Special
Agent Montana rappelling down Thomas Jefferson's
face. It was supposed to be a tongue-in-cheek homage to
Cary Grant's scene in *North by Northwest.* And Johnny
wasn't supposed to be doing the actual rappelling; there
was a stunt double on the set for that. But, like Tom
Cruise and Harrison Ford, Johnny couldn't resist taking
stunt work into his own hands. Among action stars, it
was a point of macho pride. Studio executives and insurance bonding companies hated it, but what could they
do? If Johnny Mars wanted to hang by a harness from a
six-story stone carving of a dead president's head, who
was going to say no?

Johnny had mixed up the buckles on his harness and
attached them incorrectly. Making matters worse, he
waved away a final safety check that might have caught
the error. At first, as the star was winched down the side
of the mountain, there was no sign of anything wrong. In
fact, Johnny was so coolly confident, he cracked up the
crew by pretending to pick Jefferson's nose. But, all of a
sudden, for no apparent reason, Johnny's body went slack,
his eyes rolled back in his head, and he lost consciousness. The blackout caused him to flip upside down and
his incorrectly buckled harness to snap open. He dangled

for a heart-stopping second or two with his legs caught in the rappelling ropes. Then he dropped forty feet onto an overhang under Jefferson's chin. The whole thing had been caught on camera by the film crew, including the sickening thud when Mars's body hit the ground. The only footage on CNN, though, was news chopper video of Johnny on a gurney being loaded into an ambulance. CNN was reporting that Johnny was alive, thank goodness, but had suffered unknown, potentially devastating injuries.

My phone rang. "What time do you want to leave tonight?" It was Robin, calling from her station at the reception desk, reminding me about a theater date we had for that evening. Robin and I went to lots of plays together, mostly the sort performed on tiny stages in converted basements so far off Broadway you needed a torch and compass to find them. When she wasn't answering *KNOW*'s phones, Robin was an aspiring playwright, and had aspiring actor friends workshopping shows all over town. I wasn't much of a theater buff, and ant farms were more entertaining than most of the pretentious snooze fests Robin dragged me to, but I was a fan of actresses. I'd sit in my crappy plastic folding chair in the theater and nudge Robin with my elbow whenever a girl I wanted to meet wandered onstage. "Boyfriend," she'd whisper. Or, "Crazy." Or, "Mine," if she happened to have a crush on her too.

I told Robin about Johnny's accident. "Fuck," she muttered into the phone. Then, after a moment of silence, "Have you talked to Samantha? Are you going to call her? You should call her. Or maybe send a card—a card would be nice."

"Her husband just fell off a mountain onto his head," I snapped. "I don't think Hallmark makes a card for that."

"Just let her know that you're thinking of her. That she's on your mind. That's true all the time, anyway, but she needs to know it. Jesus, what a cosmic screwing. All that money and fame and power, and something like this can still happen to you. What a story. I bet they make Johnny Mars the cover this week."

They didn't—Condoleezza Rice got the honor—but Mars did get a cover line and four pages inside the magazine. Mars was all over the front pages of the afternoon tabloid editions, however. I saw a copy of the *Post* in Carla's assistant's cubicle. MARS CRATERS! shrieked the headline. The photo was a publicity shot from one of Johnny's early Jack Montana movies, showing the ripped he-man dangling shirtless from a flagpole on top of the White House. I saw on TV that media camps had already sprung up outside the hospital in South Dakota where Mars had been taken and also at the star's apartment on the Upper West Side. I couldn't figure out why paparazzi would be gathering outside Mars's home in New York when everybody knew he was thousands of miles away. Then it hit me: they were hoping to get a good wife-in-distress shot when Sammy left the building to rush to her husband's side. There were photographers waiting for her at the airport, as well. Suddenly, Samantha was news. As far as the media was concerned, she was Johnny Mars's potential grieving widow.

I tried calling Sam but her voice mail was full. I tried writing an e-mail but my fingers froze on the keyboard. What could I possibly say to comfort her? Of course, I felt terrible about Johnny's accident, just like everyone did. Maybe even more terrible, since I was also feeling guilty. I had hated the man. I had wished evil upon him. And now evil was upon him in a way you wouldn't wish on your worst enemy. I mean, he *was* my worst enemy, and I wouldn't have wished this on him. And yet, if I had to be honest and confess my ugliest impulses, I was also wondering—I couldn't help myself—if this might be the way I was finally going to get Samantha back. That made me feel even more guilty.

Mostly, though, I was just worried about Sammy. The poor girl had to be scared out of her mind. I prayed she hadn't been watching Dr. Jordan Charles on CNN. "A fall like that could have tragic consequences," he had told Aaron Brown, stating the all too obvious. "A drop like that could easily kill a man."

"Dear Samantha," I finally tapped onto my computer screen. "I don't know what to say. Literally, I'm at a loss for words. I'm just not a good enough writer to tell you how I feel today. You know how much I care about you—you've always known—and that I'd do anything in the world for you. Please let me know if there's anything at all I can do to help. Even if all you need are arms to hug you or a shoulder to cry on . . ." I wrote a few more lines, more or less in the same vein, clicked the Send button, and headed out the office doors toward the elevator banks, where Robin intercepted me. "You're going," she said. "You *are* going."

I didn't have a choice. Even though I was in no mood to go to a play, this wasn't just any night at the theater—it was the opening of Robin's own work. No less a company than Dirty Halos, the ultra-hip acting troupe with a theater in Chelsea, was mounting a production of *You're Going to Hell, Charlie Brown,* the comic-tragic satiric masterpiece Robin had been toiling on for a year. I was going.

I had to hand it to Robin, it was a clever premise for a play: Charlie Brown and the rest of the Peanuts gang were now grown-ups in their late twenties living in New York, dealing with adult issues like binge drinking, sexual harassment, and eating disorders. Linus was a broker on Wall Street, Schroeder was the keyboardist for a Brooklyn hip-hop band, Pigpen was working for an Internet startup, and Lucy was an assistant editor at Condé Nast. But Charlie himself, now a homeless heroin addict turning tricks in the Bowery, stole the show with the darkest, funniest monologue in the play. "Good fucking grief," he told the audience as he lit a cigarette on the stage. "That little red-haired bitch stole my money! I can't stand it! I just can't stand it! AAAUUGH!" He was still wearing a yellow short-sleeved shirt with a black zigzag stripe around the middle.

"Brilliant," I told Robin as we walked down Eighth Avenue after the play to join the Dirty Halo actors at the Corner Bistro. "Honestly, Charles Schultz has to be spinning in his grave. I'm so impressed."

"You just want me to introduce you to the actress who plays Sally," Robin said, deflecting the compliment.

"Actually, the one who played Peppermint Patty was kind of cute."

"She's a lesbian," said Robin. "Only a lesbian could truly capture that character."

"Peppermint Patty was a lesbian?"

"Oh, c'mon," Robin said, looking at me like I was an idiot. "She wore Birkenstocks. She coached a softball team. How many clues do you need?"

"By the way," I asked, "where was Snoopy? How come he wasn't in the play?"

"Snoopy?" Robin answered, straight-faced. "Snoopy is dead."

Both Patty and Sally were indeed cute, and the actress playing Lucy wasn't bad either, but I hadn't nudged Robin in the ribs once during the play. I just couldn't get my mind off Mars's accident. I kept seeing the image of Johnny's body being loaded into an ambulance. I kept thinking about Samantha. I tried to recall my last conversation with her. We'd had one of our late-night chats about a month earlier. Mostly we talked about movies—she had just seen *The Dancer Upstairs,* I had just seen *Charlie's Angels: Full Throttle.* Johnny had just left to start shooting *Don't Tread on Me.* It was weird, but suddenly Sammy seemed farther out of reach than ever. Before we got to the restaurant, I made Robin wait while I tried calling Sam again on my cell phone. Her voice mail was still full. Robin put her arm around me and did her best to cheer me up. "Let's get drunk," she said.

The Corner Bistro is a hole in the wall at the corner of Jane and West Fourth Street that happens to serve New York's finest hamburgers—and cheapest beer. The place was always packed with an esoteric crowd—artists dressed like homeless people, or homeless people dressed like artists, I could never tell. The *Charlie Brown* gang took up the whole back room, where the booths were located. Robin made a beeline for Peppermint Patty. I couldn't blame her. She was an adorable pixie. The cute spray of freckles on her nose did wonders to soften the piercings on her eyebrow and lip.

After a few beers, I began to loosen up. I even tried flirting with Sally for a while, although slurring has never been my best pickup technique. Then, as was bound to happen, the subject of Johnny Mars's accident was broached. The actor doing the broaching was the guy who played Schroeder, a handsome but pompous Kevin Kline type who'd been annoying the waitress all night by barking beer orders in mock-Shakespearean oratory ("Wench, more ale, anon!"). When I first spotted him onstage crouching over his keyboards, I took an instant dislike to him.

"I worked with Johnny Mars once," the pompous guy announced to the room. "I had a role in *Rocket's Red Glare* . . ."

"Some role!" one of the other Dirty Halos interrupted, laughing. "You played a hotel bellboy. You were on-screen for two seconds . . ."

"I still worked with him," pompous guy continued.

"You didn't work with him—you worked with his *luggage* . . ."

"*Rocket's Red Glare*—is that the one where Johnny Mars throws the bad guy off the Golden Gate Bridge?" asked Sally.

"No, *Rocket's Red Glare* is the one where he throws him from the Washington Monument," Peppermint Patty said. "*Give Me Death* is the one where he throws him off the Golden Gate."

"Worst actor I've ever worked with," pompous guy continued, undeterred by the interruptions. "Seriously, the man could not remember his lines. They had to hold up idiot cards with his dialogue written on them. And that voice! Like a mouth full of wet paper towels."

"I saw him in *Coriolanus* at the Public Theater," the actress who played Marcie chimed in, pinching her nose. "I don't know why he keeps trying to be taken seriously as an actor. Isn't it enough being a movie star?"

Robin was giving me concerned glances. Listening to a bunch of downtown theatrical poseurs deride the acting chops of my ex-girlfriend's critically injured husband was not the sort of cheering up she had in mind for me. She could see that the conversation was getting on my nerves. And that I was finishing my fifth beer. "Has anybody seen *Seabiscuit* yet?" she said, changing the subject. "I hear it's really good . . ."

"A toast to Johnny Mars!" pompous guy went on, ignoring Robin. "Living proof that it's better to have luck than talent!"

"Fuck you, you pretentious shithead!" I shouted. Pompous guy wasn't saying anything I hadn't heard about Johnny Mars before—most of it I'd probably said myself. But for some reason, tonight the sentiment was making my blood boil. "I remember you in *Rocket's Red Glare*," I lied. "You sucked as a bellhop. You were the worst bellhop I've ever seen!" Robin gathered our coats and started navigating us both toward the exit as the room full of actors watched in stunned, open-jawed silence. "And you know what else?" I shouted over my shoulder as Robin shoved me out the door. "You stank as Schroeder!"

For a few silent moments, Robin and I stood outside at the corner of West Fourth and Jane. She glared at me with an expression I'd never seen on her face before. I was sure she was going to slug me. When she took a step closer, I squeezed my eyes shut and prepared for the blow. But instead all I felt were her warm arms wrapping around me, holding me tight.

9

The next time I heard Samantha's voice was at sunrise on New Year's Day, 2004, about five months after the accident. I'd spent New Year's Eve on the red-eye flying back from Los Angeles—I'd had an interview with Woody Harrelson, speaking of red eyes—and when I got home at six in the morning, the blinking light on my phone told me I had voice mail. "Hey Max," Sammy said. "I got your e-mail. Hearing from you meant a lot to me. *You* mean a lot to me. Things are so horrible right now, I can't even begin to describe it. I don't know when I'll be able to see you. But I really do want to see you. I *need* to see you . . ."

She sounded weird, like she was talking underwater, or maybe under sedation. Although, given what she'd been through over those five months, I doubted a drug had been invented that could soothe her pain.

The good news was that Johnny was alive. A few hours after the fall, he woke up in his hospital suite in South Dakota, looked at the room full of doctors and nurses, and said, "Oops." The fall obviously hadn't affected his love of a good one-liner. In fact, incredibly, miraculously, the fall had barely mussed his hair. Aside from a couple of broken ribs and a fractured collarbone, he was otherwise undented. The doctors were astonished. But then they ran a battery of tests and scans to discover what had caused Johnny to black out while rappelling in the first place. They found a tiny cancerous nodule attached to his pineal gland. That was bad news, very, very bad.

As I learned from the parade of experts making the rounds on the cable news networks, the pineal gland is the mysterious pinecone-shaped part of the brain that regulates sleep, aging, sexuality, some motor control, and, according to a growing body of scientific evidence, much of an individual's personality. Depending on how aggressive the cancer growing inside Johnny's head was, the prognosis ranged from grim to devastating. Tremors, seizures, temporary or permanent blindness, amnesia, hearing loss, personality changes, premature aging, muscle atrophy, and partial or total paralysis—this was what Johnny had to look forward to in the three, or five, or, if he was really lucky, seven years he had left to live.

According to the experts on TV, Johnny's was an incredibly rare form of brain cancer affecting fewer than one in a million people. Roughly the same statistical chances, I reckoned, for the son of an Alaskan lumberjack to come to Hollywood and end up one of the world's most famous action stars. To be chosen by fate for fame and fortune only to have all your success reduced to rubble by a tumor the size of a poppy seed—this was tragedy on a scale that would impress even ancient Greek playwrights. That the disease had been discovered thanks to a freak accident on Mount Rushmore just made the whole thing all the more appallingly bizarre and ironic.

Understandably, Mars's first impulse—or the first impulse of his management team—was to get out of the spotlight. Production on *Don't Tread on Me* was "suspended indefinitely," as the press release from the studio delicately put it. Johnny, with Sammy at his side, retreated to his Upper West Side penthouse, seldom venturing out for anything but trips to the hospital for more futile medical tests. The media, at the beginning, respected Johnny's personal space. They treated the star with kid gloves, turning his accident on Mount Rushmore into a public crusade for greater safety on movie sets. Johnny's beautiful young wife, meanwhile, was given the sobriquet "Saint Samantha," a reward for her stoicism and resolve in the face of her husband's tragic circumstances.

"Oh, shut up," Sammy said when I jokingly used the nickname during another late-night call. She started making a lot of them around that time. Sammy had always been a night owl, but since the accident she'd been having even more trouble sleeping. They were about the saddest conversations I'd ever had with another human being. "Johnny is in denial," she told me in one of them. "He really thinks he can beat this thing. But he's deteriorating every day. He sometimes gets so weak he can barely walk on his own. Just getting out of bed and into the bathroom in the morning can be a huge ordeal. One of the doctors suggested he get a wheelchair. I thought Johnny was going to slug him."

"He's got you," I told her. "He's always been lucky to have you."

"Well, he needs me now," she said. "I guess I could be grateful for that."

She was breaking my heart all over again.

You can't starve the media forever. Sooner or later the beast grows hungry. Without fresh pictures, the paparazzi eventually got more aggressive and began following Sammy whenever she left the penthouse. Without new facts, the tabloids started mixing truth with gossip. Sometimes even I had trouble telling the difference. There was a particularly nasty rumor going around, for instance, that the only reason Mars had married Samantha was that he got her pregnant, and that Sammy had miscarried a few months after their wedding. Preposterous, I thought, until I realized that the timing sort of made sense. Sammy could have been pregnant that night she turned up distraught at my door at two in the morning.

There were also rumors that Johnny was consulting with quack doctors promising to cure his cancer with "breakthrough" treatments being developed in South Korean clinics. This turned out to be true. Johnny was spending hundreds of thousands of dollars on untested experimental therapies that no Western scientist (or insurance company) would touch. Facing such a grim prognosis from his traditional-medicine doctors in New York, what did Johnny have to lose? At least the Eastern quacks offered him hope. But the press had a field day, printing made-up stories about Johnny consulting with a shaman and taking mescaline extract mixed with steroids.

The worst rumors, however, were the ones about Johnny's tumor supposedly altering his personality. From the media vantage, personality changes were one of the more sensational symptoms of having a cancer growing in your skull. So there were dozens of items in the tabloids about how Mars had become a monster at home, raging at his wife, firing household staff, making impossible demands of his doctors and nurses. The funny thing was, I knew from my phone calls with Samantha that the exact opposite was true. There had indeed been a personality change, but for the better. Sure, Johnny suffered from bouts of depression and was understandably having a hard time accepting his situation. But now that he needed Sam, he was kinder to her, softer, more loving. She certainly wasn't getting left behind with the luggage anymore.

Eventually, Mars decided to come out of hiding to "take control of his press," as publicists say. A crisis management expert was summoned and a media plan was hatched. First thing they did was hire a ghostwriter and commission a quickie memoir. It was written, printed, and in bookstores in under four months, a new publishing industry record. Then, to help plug the book, Johnny and Sammy went on a chat show charm offensive.

"Welcome back to *Larry King Live*. Joining us now from New York, Johnny Mars, actor, health activist, and author of the new memoir *Fight of My Life: How I Lived Before I Died*. With Johnny is his lovely wife, a terrific gal, Samantha Mars. Johnny will be fifty-two years old tomorrow. Happy birthday, Johnny!"

Less than a year had passed since the accident, but already Mars was a sliver of his former self. His once ruggedly handsome face was gaunt and pasty, and his thick mane of hair was beginning to thin. Even Larry King looked healthier. Sammy sat by his side, her arm hooked under his, and gazed up at her husband with Nancy Reagan eyes. She looked skinny. And tired. And not all that thrilled to be on TV.

"So, Johnny, how are you feeling these days?" King began the interview. "You look terrific!"

"I feel terrific, Larry," Johnny answered, his rumbling voice still capable of setting off seismographs. "Honestly, Larry, I feel like I'm growing stronger every day. I've changed my diet. I've been living healthier. No more cigars, isn't that right, Sammy?"

Samantha nodded and continued smiling.

"And I've been working with doctors and scientists around the world to find a cure for brain cancers of all sorts," Johnny went on. "Not just Western scientists, but also doctors of Eastern medicine. They've been making amazing advancements in brain cancer treatment in places like South Korea. We're still a long way from a cure, Larry, but there's growing hope for people like me."

"That's great, Johnny. Sammy, let me get personal with you for a minute," the talk show host said, turning his attention to my ex-girlfriend. "I'm going to ask what everyone is wondering. What about intimacy? How has all this changed your physical relationship with Johnny?" Samantha looked dumbfounded by the question, and embarrassed, but quickly recovered. "Oh, you know,

Larry," she said, laughing, "Johnny has never really needed any help in that department. He's always been *very* healthy that way."

I wanted to strangle King with his own suspenders. But I knew that Samantha was lying. She had let slip the truth during one of our late-night talks. It might have been a symptom of the cancer, or a side effect of the unorthodox treatments he was taking, but Johnny was all but dead below the waist. At first, I have to admit, that news had me cheering inside. For years the thought of that big oaf defiling my darling Samantha had been fueling my nightmares—at least that part of my torture was finally over. But then, as I thought about it more, I started to feel something odd. Something I never would have guessed I was capable of feeling. I felt sorry for the guy. The fact that Johnny Mars would never again be able to make love to my ex-girlfriend made me sad. How weird is that?

10

That fall, my dad had a heart attack. He'd been raking the backyard when a shooting pain in his chest knocked him to his knees. I got the news from the neighbor who found him in a pile of leaves, unconscious. My father was at White Plains Hospital, the neighbor told me over the phone. Alive, as far as he knew.

I hailed a yellow cab outside the *KNOW* building and had the driver take me all the way to White Plains. It was faster than the commuter train. It took a while to find his room—turned out there were two Robert Lerners listed as patients, but Dad wasn't the one having a vasectomy. He was sleeping when I tiptoed in. He looked pale as a ghost. There were tubes coming out of his nose and others going into his arm. An EKG machine beeped softly at his bedside. A doctor in green hospital scrubs gently tapped my shoulder and led me into the corridor. "He's going to be okay," he said. "It was a posterior myocardial infarction, which is bad, but not the worst kind of heart attack. We'll monitor him here for a couple of days, but he'll need help when he goes home. He'll need a nurse."

"He's going to hate that," I said. "He doesn't even like having a cleaning lady in the house."

"He's going to have to make some changes," the doctor went on. "He's going to have to change his diet and start exercising."

"He's pretty set in his ways," I said. "He's not great with change."

"How great is he with death?" the doctor asked.

I went back into Dad's room and sat in a chair for a while, watching him breathe. I realized I couldn't remember ever seeing my father sleep before. Eventually, a nurse came in to tell me visiting hours were almost up. I opened the closet door and hunted through Dad's clothes until I found his house keys. For the first time in fifteen years, I'd be spending the night in Shady Hill, in my attic room above the garage.

The ancestral abode was exactly as I remembered it. In fact, all of Shady Hill seemed frozen in time. Nothing had changed. The same picket fences around the same houses, the same well-groomed yards, the same dogwood and oak trees. In Manhattan, neighborhoods rise and fall in the span of a decade, but the suburbs are eternal.

I saw my father once or twice a year, but it was always in New York, at the Russian Tea Room or the '21' Club or one of the other antediluvian establishments he'd dined in during his Madison Avenue days. It was more comfortable for both of us. He didn't like visitors and I had zero emotional attachment to the house I grew up in. I couldn't remember the last time I'd set foot in the place. Five years? Ten? Looking around now, I noticed that Dad hadn't redecorated much. When something broke or wore out, he simply replaced it with as close a match as he could find. I don't think he was being sentimental about my mother's furniture. It was just easier to keep things the same. The only new additions to the decor were the flat-screen TV in the den that I'd sent him for Christmas two years ago and a golf putting set in the living room. I didn't even know Dad played.

Judging from the way the door stuck, my old room hadn't seen much foot traffic since the day I left for college. When I finally pried it open, I felt like I was cracking the seals on an ancient tomb. Inside were the artifacts of my teenhood, perfectly preserved through the ages. The bookshelf by the window was still filled with dog-eared Ian Fleming and Alistair MacLean paperbacks. On my desk was a first-generation Macintosh computer (I was always an early adopter), and on the wall above that was the faded blank space where I had once tacked up a Jack Montana movie poster. Dad had apparently entered the room from time to time; he had turned one corner into a storage hold. There was a stack of cardboard boxes. When I looked inside, I saw they contained every copy of *KNOW* magazine that had my byline. Dad had been collecting my stories. I sat down on the small bed. The springs creaked so loudly it startled me to my feet. Maybe I'd sleep on the sofa downstairs.

The refrigerator contained pretty much what you'd expect from the home of a widowed seventy-year-old retiree: A half-empty jar of martini olives and some old salami. Fortunately, there was also a six-pack of beer. I was about to open one when I heard a short burst of musical beeps—was that "Swanee River"?—coming from the basement. How weird. Like every idiot victim in every cheesy slasher film I'd ever seen, I opened the basement door and slowly stepped down the stairs. Except there wasn't a serial killer in a hockey mask waiting for me. Dad had recently bought a new clothes dryer that played a little ditty to let you know its drying cycle was done, and then repeated it every thirty minutes until the dryer was shut off. Dad had obviously been doing a load of laundry while raking the backyard. I had to give the guy credit for keeping busy.

I shut off the dryer, but before I climbed back up the stairs, I happened to glance over at Dad's workshop table. There were bundles of old letters scattered on its surface. They were all in my mother's soft, flowing hand. I picked one up and noted the date—January 16, 1967—three years before my birth. Some were dated earlier, others later. I sat down on a stool and started reading. What was in them wasn't always very interesting. The letters written during their courtship were filled with minutiae about rendezvous arrangements at train stations and airports—the sort of details modern-day lovers send via text message. But there were also anniversary cards and birthday poems and other corny notes scribbled after they were well into their marriage, before my mother's car accident. Next to the table, there was a dusty trunk filled with even more letters. It broke my heart. After all those years since her death, Dad still climbed down into the basement to spend time with Mom.

I decided to get out of the house for some fresh air before the sun set. Without really thinking about it, I found myself taking a stroll down memory lane—literally. I walked the six blocks to Sammy's old house, where her parents still lived. I knew the route so well I could have made the trip with my eyes closed and walking backward.

I hesitated before ringing the bell. I couldn't remember the last time I'd seen Sammy's parents. I wasn't sure how they'd feel about a blast from their daughter's past turning up on their doorstep, but I needn't have worried. "Oh, come in, come in!" Sam's mom said, as if she'd been expecting me. The house was still a study in chaos. A cat zoomed out the door, pursued by a dog. Another cat was playing a free-form jazz tune by walking on the piano keys in the living room. Sammy's dad was sitting on a La-Z-Boy in the den, watching an old *I Spy* rerun on TV. We had always bonded over our mutual love of crappy espionage shows (and of his daughter). Nothing had changed here, either. Until I looked a bit closer. There were framed pictures of Sammy and Johnny all over the place. I also noticed that the bookshelves in the den, which used to be cluttered with unread Book-of-the-Month Club editions, now held a tidy row of neatly labeled DVD cases. "Sammy Age 12," one of them was marked. "Sammy skiing in Vermont," said another. They looked brand-new.

"*20/20* is doing an interview with Samantha next month and they went through all our home movies looking for footage of her as a kid," Sam's dad explained when he saw me checking out the DVDs. "We gave them boxes and boxes of old videotape I found in our attic, and they brought us back these. They practically indexed every frame. Want to see one?" I had a private coronary while I tried to remember what Sammy did with a particular home video we'd made together in college, but was quickly distracted by the scene that sparkled to life on the TV screen. It was an image of ten-year-old Sammy at a beach, trying to coax her younger sister into the waves. "Cape Cod," her dad said. "Summer of 1980."

"Show him the prom," Sammy's mom said, laughing. "That one is priceless."

Sammy's dad switched discs and there we were— Sammy and me at eighteen, standing in her parents' driveway in front of a hired limo. I was going through a punk stage and had on a midnight blue tuxedo, a black ruffled shirt, and a red skinny tie. Sammy had squirted enough petroleum jelly in my hair to fill the *Exxon Valdez* and had given me a spiky 'do that she thought was trendy. I looked like Sid Vicious on the way to a black-tie circus. But Sammy was beautiful in the cream-colored silk gown she had borrowed from her older sister. Fifteen years later, sitting in her parents' den, I couldn't take my eyes off her. "This isn't going to turn up on *20/20,* is it?" I asked her dad.

"No, I'm saving this one in case we ever need to blackmail you."

"Dad, you're not dying."

"How do you know?" my father asked, adjusting the

angle of his hospital bed with the remote control for the fiftieth time that morning. The tubes were gone from his nose and arm and the color had returned to his face. But he was sure he was a goner.

"Because the doctors say you'll be fine," I told him. "You need rest and a proper diet. And a nurse. We have to find you a nurse."

"I don't need a nurse," he said. "I need a funeral director. I'm not making it out of this room alive . . ."

"Dad, if you don't knock it off with the adjustable bed, I'll make sure you need a funeral director. Give me that thing."

I loved the guy—he was my dad—but he drove me nuts. Not to be disloyal to my mom, but I think even she would have wished that he'd fallen in love and remarried after her death. Twenty-five years of solitary widowerhood had made him as sad and hard as a gravestone. He still hadn't gotten over her. He brought her up every time we spoke. Granted, Mom was pretty much the only thing we had in common, especially after I left the house to make my way in the world, but the truth was I barely remembered her. All I had were fleeting sensory ghosts. The sound of her laughing. The softness of her hair. The warmth of her touch. I was only eight when she died. I hardly knew her.

"You look more and more like her every year," my dad said.

"Dad, please," I said, rolling my eyes.

"That's a compliment, kid. Your mother was a beautiful woman. You know she was in *Life* magazine—"

"In a toothpaste advertisement, I know," I interrupted

him. "Dad, look, I went down into the basement yesterday, and I saw the letters."

"You're snooping around in my house?" He grabbed the remote out of my hand and raised the back of the bed in order to confront me. The adjustment took several seconds, somewhat undercutting the effect. "I don't snoop around in your house! Why are you snooping in mine?"

"I was turning off the dryer—it kept beeping at me. And I saw the letters. I'm concerned about you, Dad. It's not healthy. Mom's been gone a long time. You really need to let her go. Maybe even meet someone else. It's not too late."

"Ha!" he snorted. "That's funny. I'm seventy years old. I'm not about to start picking up chicks at discotheques. No, Max, I made my choice. I chose your mother. It was the best choice I ever made, no matter what happened. But look who's talking! What about you? When are you going to make a choice? You're thirty-one years old—"

"Thirty-four," I corrected him.

"That's what I'm saying. You're in your mid-thirties and you still haven't found the right girl."

"How do you know I haven't found her?" I said. "Maybe I have found her but just can't have her. Maybe I had her but she was taken from me."

"That girl who married the movie star? The one who lived down the street? Samantha?"

I nodded.

"She made her choice, Max, and it wasn't you. That means she wasn't the right girl." He motioned me to come closer. "Find the right girl, son. She's out there somewhere. Just open your eyes." He reached up and affectionately ruffled my hair, just like he did when I was a boy. Then he started playing with the bed's remote control again.

A few days later, I got a late-night call from Samantha. Her parents must have told her about my father being sick. "I'm so sorry," she said. "I hope he's doing better. Remember when we were fifteen and he drove us to that Duran Duran concert and spent the whole night sitting in the car in the parking lot? The poor guy. I always felt bad for him. He never got over your mom."

"Well, you know, we Lerner men—we mate for life," I said.

We talked for an hour, our longest conversation in months, and would have talked longer except Sammy had to catch a flight in the morning to Wyoming. They were selling the ranch—the bills from Korean doctors were piling up—and she needed to be there to close the deal. But we arranged to have dinner when she got back to New York, just like old times. It would be our first meeting since before Johnny got diagnosed with brain cancer.

11

"Nine, four, four, double-B, D, C," Samantha said.

"Pardon?" I replied.

"Nine, four, four, double-B, D, C," she repeated, flustered and irritated. "That's the license plate of the black SUV that's circling the block right now. It followed me to the restaurant. It's a photographer. He goes wherever I go, day and night. He's made Johnny his specialty. Except Johnny hardly ever leaves the apartment, so he ends up taking three hundred pictures of me every day."

We had just settled into a booth at a restaurant on Eighth Avenue in the Theater District, not far from *KNOW*'s offices. Holiday decorations were up all over the city. The tree at Rockefeller Center was sparkling with shiny balls. The Cartier Building was wrapped in a giant red ribbon. The mannequins in Barneys' windows were strangling each other with Christmas lights. And the Italian bistro where Sammy and I were meeting had hung sprigs of mistletoe above all the tables. I pointed ours out to Sammy as she slipped out of her coat. She smiled and planted a kiss on my cheek. Then she continued on about the photographer in the SUV.

"The weird thing is," she said, "I never see the guy's face. All I ever see is his camera lens sticking out from the car window. Just once, I'd like to look him in the eye."

She was as lovely as ever. She had the same warm smile, the same soft laugh, the same irresistibly kissable lips. But I couldn't help noticing something about her eyes—remoteness, perhaps, or loneliness—that hadn't been there before. After all the stress and horror she'd endured over the last year and a half, I wouldn't have been surprised if she had shown up for our dinner with white hair and a facial tic. One minute Sammy was the carefree bride of a matinee idol, jetting from topless beaches in the Mediterranean to mountaintop ski resorts in the Alps. The next, she found herself trapped in a world of bedpans and bedsores, the stoical wife of the most famous terminal case on the planet. It couldn't have been more tragically ironic if Rod Serling had written it.

"How's Johnny doing?" I asked after the waiter finished filling our wineglasses with merlot.

"Great," Sam said, taking a long sip. "In fact, the doctors say . . ." Her eyes met mine and she couldn't finish the sentence. She sighed. "The truth is," she said, "he's terrible. He takes all these weird medicines from these strange doctors, and he does all these exercises, physical therapy that's supposed to help stop the muscles from atrophying. But none of it works." Sammy took another big sip. "To make things even worse, his family from Alaska has moved in. They said they wanted to help, but all they do is ask how much things are worth. It's like they're taking inventory for when he dies. I've caught them going through our drawers and cabinets. They're so . . ." Sammy stopped again and took a deep, Zen breath. "I'm sorry," she said, forcing herself to smile. "Let's start over. I'm being a drag. I don't want to be a drag. I just want to have a good time tonight. Let's just have fun, okay?"

And so we did. We drained the whole bottle of merlot, then ordered another, while I did everything short of sticking straws up my nose to make Sammy laugh. I regaled her with tales of my dating misadventures. I had her rolling on the floor with stories about my experiences in Hollywood. We reminisced over shared childhood memories, about our secret sleepovers during high school, and our over-the-top melodramatic separations during college. We had so much fun, we didn't notice that hours had passed. When I looked up to pay the bill, I saw that we were the only ones left in the restaurant. Our waiter was standing at the bar, looking resentful. Sammy took out her little silver RAZR cell phone and started tapping at its keypad. "I'm sending a message to my driver," she said. "I'm asking him if the photographer in the SUV is still there." A few seconds later, she got the response. "Damn," Sam said. "Still there." She looked around the restaurant until her eyes stopped at the entrance to the kitchen. "Come on," she said, grabbing my hand. "Let's make a break for it."

We got some startled glances from the busboys cleaning up the prep tables and mopping the floor, but as luck would have it there was a back door in the kitchen that led to an alleyway outside. "I don't want to go home yet," Sammy said, stepping over some garbage bags. We were both a little tipsy, but I don't think it was the wine that was making Samantha drunk. I think it was the freedom. "Your office is around here somewhere, isn't it?" she asked. "Let's go to your office. I want to see where you work!"

It had started to snow—flakes as big as cotton balls floated all around us as we wobbled up Broadway. It made the city look like one of Carla's globes. I swiped my ID card at the entrance of the *KNOW* building and we stumbled into the empty lobby, making our way to the elevators. Like naughty children, we skulked through the magazine's darkened halls, the judgmental eyes of politicians and celebrities gazing down at us from the blown-up covers framed along the walls. I fumbled with my keys, opened my office door, and switched on just the desk lamp to give the room a warm, cozy glow. My eyes followed Samantha around the room as she examined the pop culture treasures I'd picked up over the years. She yanked the string on my talking Ed Grimley doll ("I must say!"). She stroked my Tribble. She accidentally set off the ejector roof on the tiny James Bond car sitting on my bookshelf, sending the little plastic guy in the passenger seat flying under my desk. Sam and I bumped heads when we both bent down to retrieve him. When we stood up, our faces were so close I could feel her breath on my lips.

For a heartbeat, it seemed as if no time had passed since her dad had videotaped us as teenagers in our prom outfits, since we lived together in that tiny apartment in the West Village, since before Johnny Mars came into her life and ruined mine.

Just when I decided to lean in even closer, Sammy

spotted something on a shelf that made her jaw drop. She shot me an astonished look, then reached for the familiar-looking green ceramic turtle-shaped penny bank she made in fourth grade. I'd never been able to throw the thing away. She turned it over in her hands and ran a finger along the initials she had carved into the turtle's foot as a little girl. Her eyes filled with tears.

"I can't believe you've kept this thing," she said.

"Well," I responded, trying to make light of it, "it's still got money in it."

Samantha put the turtle back on the shelf and leaned into me for a long, warm hug. When she looked up, I could tell from her expression what was coming next. "I better get going," she whispered softly. "I don't want to, but I really should. I've probably stayed too long already." She ran her fingers through my hair. Finally, she peeled herself from my arms and straightened her dress, and we walked back to the elevators. I pushed the button labeled "L," for "Loser."

12

I always get lost at Heathrow Airport. I follow the signs and remember to walk on the left side of the corridors, but inevitably I take a wrong turn and end up emerging out of a drainage pipe in Slough.

I had arrived at Heathrow in early 2005 to begin my most ambitious journalistic endeavor to date—or at least my biggest boondoggle. My plan was to circumnavigate the globe on the trade winds of publicity, stopping to interview film stars and visit movie sets in London, Paris, Rome, Prague, and finally, heading much farther east, Cambodia, where DeeDee Devry would throw herself at me in a wet bedsheet before I returned to New York by way of LA. When I proposed the three-week jaunt to my editor, Carla, she barely batted an eye. "Bring me back some snow globes," she said.

More and more, my comfort zone was shifting from life on Earth to life in the clouds. Air travel was like putting the world on pause. So long as I was in transit, nothing could touch me. Not even Samantha. Especially not

Samantha. Of course, there were drawbacks. It was sometimes crushingly lonely. One year, I had Thanksgiving dinner alone at thirty thousand feet over Greenland. Another
year I celebrated my birthday at a duty-free airport shop
in Australia. Most people measure the milestones of their
lives with events like marriages and births. My landmarks
were the trips I took and the stars I interviewed. Rowing
a kayak in Sydney Harbor with Russell Crowe. Clinking
glasses of aquavit in Oslo with Tom Cruise. Those were
my Kodak moments. I'd be collecting a bunch more of
them on this journey around the world.

I finally found my way to the Heathrow Express
to London. As the train whooshed along the tracks, I
watched English shrubbery fly past my window. Then
I opened one of my bags and retrieved a fat manila file
filled with clippings on Gwen Swallow, the forty-year-
old BAFTA-winning actress who, until recently, had been
married to the renowned Shakespearean actor and director Rufus Armitage. The divorce had been nasty, with the
brunt of the bad publicity falling on the husband, who,
according to Fleet Street stories in my folder, had fled
the marriage after Gwen adopted her ninth child, a six-
month-old Tibetan girl Gwen renamed Prunella. DEAD-
BEAT DAD! booed a headline in *The Sun* over a story that
asked readers the question, "Why would a man abandon
his wife and nine children?" There was a full-page spread
of paparazzi shots showing Armitage loading the trunk
of his Jaguar outside the couple's Kensington town house.

When I got to my hotel in Knightsbridge. there was
a message waiting for me at the front desk. Swallow's
publicist wanted to change the location of the inter-

view tomorrow. Instead of tea at the Dorchester, Gwen
wanted to meet in Kensington Gardens, at a spot called
Round Pond. A curious choice—most stars tend to
avoid publicly exposed settings. But then Gwen had a
way of keeping people at bay. She could seem incredibly
approachable on stage and screen—her portrayal of a
deaf chambermaid in Mike Leigh's *Sad, Sadder, Saddest*
made millions of moviegoers want to hug her—but in
person she was as accessible as an iceberg. The regal pos-
ture, the posh Sloaney accent, the thin dismissive smile—
they all worked like a force field to keep the world at a
distance.

With the help of a tourist map, I found Round Pond
and arrived for the interview fifteen minutes early. Gwen
couldn't have picked a more idyllic London backdrop for
my story. While I waited, I soaked in the scenery. School-
boys in blue blazers and striped ties strolled the fiercely
manicured lawns. In the distance, a red double-decker bus
puttered past the ornate park gates. At the edge of the
pond, an old woman fed bread crumbs to the most enormous swans I'd ever seen. Seriously, they looked big enough
to saddle. It was all so serenely civilized, so *veddy* English,
I half expected Mary Poppins to come floating down from
the chim-chim-i-neys. Instead, on the horizon, I spotted
Gwen and her entourage marching in my direction. She
had brought the entire brood, all nine children, along with
a caravan of nannies and nurses and other assistants lug-
ging strollers and diaper bags and picnic baskets. Gwen was
wearing so many scarves and shawls, she looked like a Bed-
ouin. Her small army of children was running and shouting
in circles around her. Even the swans stopped to stare.

"So very nice to meet you," she said as she presented me with her hand. I wasn't sure if I was supposed to kiss it, or maybe curtsey before it. I just gave it a shake. As we introduced ourselves, I felt a tug at my shoulder bag and looked down to see one of Gwen's kids, a five-year-old Armenian adoptee, poking his nose into my satchel. Then he started digging out my notes and throwing them all over the lawn. A nanny attempted to distract him. "Now, Cedric, those don't belong to you." I spotted another nanny wrestling with a three-year-old Malawian boy who wanted to swim naked in the pond. "Now, Ridgewell, put your trousers on . . ." Gwen was oblivious to the mayhem. An assistant unfolded a cashmere Laura Ashley picnic blanket on the ground, and we sat down for our interview.

"I understand you are going to make another movie with Mike Leigh," I began. "What's it about?"

"Oh yes, indeed," Gwen answered. "I'll play a blind Croatian fishmonger whose husband is killed by a land mine." A swan ran behind the actress, honking in terror, pursued by a six-year-old Mongolian girl named Felicity waving a bouquet of swan feathers in her fist. "It's a heart-breaking story," she went on, undistracted, "about man's inhumanity to man . . ."

I knew the answer to *The Sun*'s rhetorical question. If I'd been married to this woman, I probably would have left her, too.

"Court-a-nee, she iz not 'ere. Ze show, eet aas been can-sealed." This late-breaking news was delivered by a French doorman at the entrance of a Paris nightclub called Espace

Cadet, where nineteen-year-old pop sensation–turned–
movie star Courtney Howell was scheduled to tape a
French TV special in front of a crowd of adoring, gyrat-
ing Parisian partygoers. Afterward, she was scheduled to
sit down for an interview with me. But Courtney hadn't
shown up. Outside the club, in the rain, clusters of dejected
fans lingered under umbrellas, looking *très misérables*.

This sometimes happened with celebrities, especially
young ones in the first dizzying flush of celebrity. When
you're not yet twenty years old, suddenly famous, and taking your first trip to an exotic city like Paris, remembering your press appointments isn't exactly a high priority.
Still, forgetting to show up for an expensively produced
TV special, leaving hundreds of teenagers disappointed,
along with a reporter from a major American magazine,
that was pretty extreme. Court-a-nee's pooblazeest, she
had explaining to do.

"It was a combination of jet lag and exhaustion," the
New York flack apologized on the phone the following
morning. "Courtney feels just terrible about it. Can we
reschedule for later today? She's supposed to be taping a
French MTV segment on a boat on the Seine. Maybe you
could do the interview then?"

A boat on the Seine sounded like a fine place to interview the Alabama-born pop tart who just a year earlier
had taken the music world by storm with her hit video
"Noxious," in which she sang and danced in a toxic waste
dump. Her recent appearance at the MTV video awards—
where she trapezed over the audience onto the stage—had
been a sensation, upstaging even Britney Spears, who
that night had merely made out with Betty White. The

movie Courtney was about to begin shooting in France—her first feature film—was *Nap and Jo,* a poppy musical about the romance between Napoléon Bonaparte and his true love, Joséphine. The Seine seemed like a fitting venue for our chat. But when I turned up at the river, Courtney was nowhere in sight. I'd been blown off again.

"She feels just awful about it," her publicist told me over the phone the next morning. "She had a terrible migraine and couldn't get out of bed. But she really wants the interview to happen. Can you meet her this afternoon at the Eiffel Tower?"

Courtney didn't show up at the Eiffel Tower. Or at the Louvre. Or the Arc de Triomphe. Or any of the other Parisian landmarks her publicist picked for our interview. Clearly, something was wrong. Perhaps the young starlet had a drug problem. Or was in the midst of a mental breakdown. Or else the sudden rush of fame had just been too much for her. Whatever was going on with Courtney Howell, alarm bells started ringing in the reporter part of my brain.

The day I was leaving for Rome, just a few hours before my flight, the interview finally happened. We conducted it at the superluxe Plaza Athénée, in the Royal Suite, a four-thousand-square-foot two-bedroom architectural ode to excess filled with stunning French antiques, embroidered silk drapes, and Italian marble mosaics. Blaring from a fancy Bose stereo was a track from the new CD Courtney would be releasing in a few months, a sexy dance tune called "Contaminated." You couldn't say she didn't have a theme. Scattered around the vast living room were garment bags packed with priceless French fashions, most delivered gratis by their designers, each hoping Courtney would be photographed wearing his label. That's one of the ironies of celebrity: The famous can buy whatever they want, but people keep giving them stuff for free. On an armchair in the corner was the script for *Nap and Jo,* along with some biographies of Joséphine de Beauharnais and a book of vocal exercises Courtney's dialect coach must have given her.

Courtney, it turned out, hadn't stepped foot outside of the suite since checking in ten days ago.

"I know I should be really excited about all this—being in Paris and making my first movie and all," she said in an accent as thick as grits. "But to tell you the truth, I'm really homesick. I miss my dogs. I miss my mom. I miss Alabama." She began biting at her fingernails, which had been nibbled to stubs. "Honestly, I don't know how I'm going to survive three whole months here. I wish I'd never agreed to make this movie. It's making me miserable and we haven't even started shooting it yet. I just want to go home."

I couldn't help myself. I actually felt bad for the kid. Not too many years ago she'd been playing with dolls. Now she practically was one, trapped in a $15,000 a night Barbie dream house.

In Rome, even the cab drivers have a certain dolce vita pizzazz. The one who picked me up at Leonardo da Vinci Airport wore a white silk scarf that flapped rakishly out the car window as he sped along the E80 toward the city's center. When we circled the Trevi Fountain near my hotel, I wanted to lean out my own window and shout "*Ciao, baby!*" to the whole gorgeous town. Visiting Rome always made me feel like Marcello Mastroianni.

On this trip, I'd be interviewing Leonard Cox on the set of *The Halo Helix,* a religious techno-thriller with a high-concept hook that was getting the actor in trouble with the same critics who would later demand that Tom Hanks be excommunicated for *The Da Vinci Code*. Leonard was playing a handsome young Vatican priest who discovers a secret plot to resurrect the body of Jesus Christ by cloning fossilized DNA discovered in the recently unearthed Tomb of Talpiot, the burial ground where Jesus' body is believed to be interred. The experiment goes horribly awry, naturally, and the replicated Christ takes off on a murderous rampage. Not surprisingly, the real Catholic Church had already condemned the film as blasphemy and a boycott was being organized in America, even though nobody outside the production company had yet to see a minute of footage.

"I don't understand why everyone is so upset, I really don't," Leonard said, chain-smoking cigarettes in his trailer at Cinecittà Studios. He was dressed in full priestly regalia, including a clerical cassock and cape, and a black cap with a pom-pom on top. A few of his character's props—a gold cross, a leather Bible, a vile of Jesus' chromosomes—were on the coffee table, along with Leonard's script pages and several empty bottles of Rossa Toro, an Italian energy drink.

Famously brainy, Leonard had dropped out of Har-

vard Law School to pursue an acting career, and suc-
ceeded brilliantly. But when it came to people skills, he
was considered to be kind of an imbecile. He not only
waged creative battles with his directors and producers,
but also with set designers and costumers and even the
craft services caterers. Screenwriters particularly hated his
guts—along with rewriting his own lines, Leonard would
take it upon himself to rewrite everyone else's, too. His
meddling added months to production schedules and millions to budgets. But his movies usually made money, and
were always critically applauded. Journalists loved the
guy. You could turn on your recorder, go out for a cup of
coffee, and when you returned an hour later you'd have
a tape full of killer material. "These Catholic protest-
ers," Leonard went on, "what's their beef? We're making
a movie here. Just a movie. But they're acting like we're
molesting baby Jesus, for Christ's sake. Like we're finger-
fucking the Virgin Mary . . ."

   After the interview, I took a long stroll through Rome,
making stops at the usual tourist traps. The Colosseum.
The Pantheon. The Spanish Steps. The ancientness of the
city put me in a pensive mood. If I'd been born here two
thousand years ago, I asked myself, what sort of person
would I have been? A scribbler of scrolls, perhaps? An
interviewer of ancient Roman celebrities? Tell me, Plau-
tus, what's your new play about? Marcus Aurelius, if you
were a tree, what sort of tree would you be? Forget two
thousand years. I'd been born just thirty-five years ago,
and I still wasn't sure what sort of person I was. I wondered if this was what I was going to be doing for the
rest my life, hopping from city to city, making the air my

home, turning myself into the *Flying Dutchman* of the 747 fleet.

The funny thing about watching stuff blow up on a soundstage is that it's almost always boring. Film crews make a big fuss about it, passing out foam earplugs and ostentatiously shouting "Fire in the hole!" before rolling the cameras. But it inevitably involves hours of tedious waiting as safeties are checked and double-checked, and the blast, when it finally goes off, never looks or sounds as fiery as it seems on the screen. Besides, on the film set I was visiting in Prague—a $100 million Jerry Bruckheimer action movie called *Boom!*—I would have been better off saving the earplugs for the dialogue.

Not that I was complaining. Prague was one of my favorite spots behind the old Iron Curtain. I loved the city's ancient clock towers and stone bridges, not to mention its dirt-cheap beer and delightfully seedy all-night casinos (one of my favorites was located right next door to the Museum of Communism). Also, I had a particular interest in *Boom!*'s leading man, Chuck Fuse, the twenty-nine-year-old ex–X Game champion who was transitioning into acting. He certainly had the hair for a big-screen career— an overgrown pompadour so wavy his stylists probably needed Dramamine to brush it. There were rumors that Fuse was being considered to replace Johnny Mars as Jack Montana. Nobody at the studio would say so in print— nobody wanted to appear callous, especially as Mars continued to deteriorate—but the franchise must go on. Obviously, a hit with *Boom!* wouldn't hurt Fuse's odds.

Before taking off on my grand tour of Europe, I'd had lunch with a studio executive at Elaine's in New York. When he suggested that replacing Mars with Fuse would be an opportunity to "reboot" the series and make it more "relevant" for younger audiences, I wanted to smash his face in with my tape recorder. I reminded the exec that the last Jack Montana movie had grossed $340 million domestically, whereas Fuse had yet to earn enough to pay for a Metro Card. I wasn't sure why, but since Johnny got sick, I'd been feeling strangely protective of my girlfriend-stealing nemesis. Maybe it was because his illness made him less threatening. Or maybe it was because it's difficult to stay mad at someone who has a terminal disease—death has a way of making everything else seem petty. Or maybe it was because you never get over your first screen idol. No matter how much I hated him, a tiny part of me couldn't help but continue to worship the guy.

Don't get me wrong—I was still in love with Johnny's wife. I still secretly fantasized about winning Samantha back. But I could no longer cast myself as David up against Goliath. Now I was slinging rocks at a guy with a brain tumor. No matter how hard I tried, I couldn't figure out how to give the fantasy a happy ending. Say, for instance, Sammy hadn't spotted that ceramic turtle in my office the night we snuck away from the paparazzo. Suppose I had leaned in for a kiss, and she had kissed me back. What then? Somehow, I couldn't see Sammy leaving her husband for me. As much as I wanted Sammy, Johnny needed her. Did I really want to be the guy who stole the wife of a dying man? Could I live with myself? Could Sammy love such a person? It was all enough to make my head explode.

I arrived at Barrandov Studios in Prague just in time for the first detonation of the day. Everybody was stuffing foam into their ears while Fuse, wearing a Navy SEAL wet suit and carrying a bazooka, took his position on the set, crouching behind a prop tree from where he would fire a prop rocket and blow up a prop Hummer full of prop terrorists. But as I put foam into my ears and braced for the explosion, I spotted something out of the corner of my eye. I saw a girl perched on a stack of boxes near some video monitors, her nose buried in a thick book. The detonation was seconds away, but I couldn't stop staring. She was wearing slim-fitting jeans and a snugly tapered white cotton blouse, with the bottom buttons left undone. A lock of honey-blond hair kept falling into her eyes, which she absently swatted away. For once, the explosion really was a doozy, but I barely noticed it. As if in slow motion, the breeze from the blowback caught the girl's shirttails, flapped them open for an instant, and exposed her bare belly button. My blood jumped.

Traditionally, on most movie sets, the only women I found that interesting were the ones with above-the-title credits. But I decided to approach the girl with the book. "What are you reading?" I asked her. She looked up at me with the greenest eyes I'd ever seen and stared coolly at my face for a long, appraising beat. Then, without uttering a word, she handed me her book. The title was in Czech but I recognized the author. She was reading Hannah Arendt. "Wow," I said. "That's heavy stuff. 'The banality of evil' and all that." That was all I knew about Hannah Arendt. The girl wasn't impressed. "We are not supposed to talk to you," she said in a sexy Slavic accent. "We were told not to talk to the reporter from America." She didn't seem worried about getting in trouble; just annoyed that her reading had been interrupted. Czechs, incidentally, do annoyed better than anybody in Europe, even the French.

Just then, a Czech production assistant with a clipboard came jogging toward us. He too seemed annoyed. "Eliska," he said, *"Chuck tě potřebuje k tlumočeni!"* The two exchanged increasingly exasperated Czech banter for a while, both of them waving their arms and rolling their eyes, then the girl turned back to me. "Excuse me," she said, gathering her belongings and stuffing them into an oversize handbag. "I cannot talk any longer. Mr. Fuse needs translating. Again." She and the production assistant rushed off, leaving me standing by myself. But I had her name! Eliska. Even better, I still had her book!

It had been a long time since just meeting a woman had triggered such a powerful physiological reaction in me. Rapid breathing. Increased pulse rate. Sweaty palms. Either I liked this girl or I was in the midst of some sort of cardiac episode. But I had to get back to work, so, for the time being, I slipped her book into my shoulder bag and turned my attention back to the set, where Chuck Fuse was standing in a wet suit waiting to shoot the rest of his action scene. He had one line, which he was supposed to deliver in front of the smoldering remains of the Hummer he'd just blown up: "Hope you've got insurance." But the actor was having trouble getting the Czech makeup artist to understand his instructions—he needed Eliska to tell him the Czech words for "more fake blood"—and the sequence dragged on for three hours, with Fuse doing take after take of the line reading. Getting the bon mots just right, he knew, would be critical to his chances of landing Johnny's old job.

The next day, I interviewed Fuse in his trailer. It was decked out with all the usual movie star gear—a plasma TV with a portable DVD player, a mini kitchen with a fully stocked fridge, a separate bedroom for quick naps (or whatever) between scenes—along with some homey touches Fuse had added himself. Tacked up to one wall was the prototype of the *Boom!* one-sheet, which featured a photograph of Fuse's naked, sweaty torso, with a mushroom cloud from an atomic bomb blast tattooed on his chest. "It's a fake tattoo," the actor said, pulling up his wife-beater to reveal a ripped but blank torso. "It was just for the poster. It took them five hours to paint it on me, and another hour to remove it. But it's way cool, isn't it? I'm thinking of getting it done for real."

After talking about acting for a while—"I just go by instinct, dude, I don't believe in studying"—I decided to ask Fuse about fame. It had been a while since I'd grilled a celebrity on the subject. "Dude, I was destined to be famous," he said, pulling a plastic comb from his pocket and raking it through the Jeff Koons sculpture that was his hairdo. "I was famous in the womb. People keep asking if I've changed since becoming a big star. But I haven't changed because I always thought of myself as a big star. It was the rest of the world that hadn't caught up to me." It was an interesting notion. Maybe some people were born with the fame gene. Like race or sexual orientation or X-Men mutations, it's simply who you are, and there isn't anything you can do about it. Perhaps it's why some people are drawn to crowds and cameras while others shrink away. On the other hand, maybe Fuse was just an egotistical boob.

Normally, with my interview done, I would have left the

set and done some sightseeing. But I still had Eliska's book. I found her sitting at the same stack of boxes near the video monitor, looking dejected. "Were you looking for this?" I said, handing over her Hannah Arendt. She let out a cheery cry. "Oh, thank God," she said. "All my notes are inside." She flipped the pages to show me the tiny Czech chicken scrawl filling up nearly every margin. "It's for school. I have an exam coming up." Now that I had rescued her from flunking twentieth-century postwar European philosophy, Eliska seemed slightly more interested in talking to me. But only slightly. Before she disappeared again, I had just enough time to learn that she was a graduate school student at Charles University and was paying her bills by working as a translator on American movie sets in Prague.

"I'm not really interested in film," she told me, her Slavic accent reminding me of every TV spy girl I'd lusted after as a teenager. "Not Hollywood movies, anyway. But I earn enough money translating on one movie set to last me most of the year."

"Would you like to have a cup of coffee with me after you're done here tonight?" I asked her. I figured I had one more evening in Prague before I headed on to Cambodia, so why not give it a shot. "We could talk about Hannah Arendt if you want," I added. "I happen to be an expert on Hannah Arendt."

"Really?" she asked, cocking an eyebrow. "You are an expert on *The Origins of Totalitarianism*?"

"Well, no," I said. "I just said that so you'd have coffee with me."

Eliska looked at me for a long moment, trying to figure out whether I was charming or just an idiot. Then she cracked up. For the time being, she was giving me the benefit of the doubt. "Okay," she said. "We can have coffee."

We did not have coffee. Instead, we met later that evening in a bar in Old Town Square and sipped Becherovka, a disgusting Czech aperitif that tastes like shag carpet and Sterno. One of the advantages of being a professional journalist is that you get lots of practice asking strangers questions. Frankly, it was one of the main things I had going for me when out on a date. Most men jaw on about themselves, trying to impress women with puffed-up tales of their conquests and achievements. But the smarter way to attract the female is to let her do all the talking. Ask a lot of questions. Feign interest. Works like a charm.

With Eliska, though, it was not so easy. Like many beautiful women—and Eliska was stunning, with cheekbones that could make a supermodel weep—she had a lot of practice deflecting attention, especially from men. At first, conversation with her was like waging a verbal siege. Whatever line I tried to fling over her ramparts came bouncing off her walls without making the slightest dent. It was only after she had a couple of glasses of Sterno and shag carpet that I began to detect the cracks in her fortifications. "Don't tell anyone," she admitted, "but I'm not the greatest translator in the world. This is only the second movie set I've worked on. I don't have the personality for it. I get too nervous and I screw up all the time." As if on cue, she knocked over the vase on the tabletop while pulling off her sweater. "Ugh," she said. "I am an elephant in Chinatown!"

Eventually, I was able to tease out some details about

her life. I learned that she was twenty-eight and grew up in a small village in rural Czechoslovakia. That her father left her mother when Eliska was a year old. That her mom ended up working night shifts as a receptionist in a state coal mine. "You know," she told me after her third Becherovka, "when I was a child, we thought America was so wonderful. It seemed so big and glamorous and far away. In fact, the word we used for 'cool' was 'America.' If somebody was wearing a cool T-shirt, we'd say, 'Wow, that T-shirt is so *America*.' Now, of course," she added with a smile, "we know better. Now everybody *hates* America."

Later on in the evening, I learned that there was even some Cold War intrigue in Eliska's family history: When she was seven years old, her mother got her heart broken by a man who ended up defecting to West Germany. "But he sent us such magnificent gifts," Eliska said, smiling. "He once sent me a denim catsuit. We couldn't get real denim under the Communist regime. Only this cheap imitation stuff. But that catsuit was very cool. It had an ABBA patch on the back pocket. All my friends were jealous."

"So America," I said.

Growing up behind the Iron Curtain, I quickly discovered, had left Eliska with some enormous pop-cultural gaps. There was a vast swath of pre-Glasnost entertainment that had literally been walled off from her childhood. *The Monkees, The Brady Bunch, Gilligan's Island*—none of them rang a bell with her. "When I was a kid, my mother and I would sometimes watch *Dynasty,* when the signal would drift over the border from the west," she offered. "We didn't know what they were saying—it was dubbed in German—but we loved it. We even loved the commercials."

To be fair, I wasn't exactly an expert on Czech pop culture. Eliska told me about the films she grew up with, ethereal, timeless fairy tales with titles like *The Proud Princess* and *Three Nuts for Cinderella*. She tried to explain the "Mister Egg" advertisements of her childhood, a Communist-era TV campaign for state-produced farm products that featured a dapper animated chicken egg in a top hat, but it had as much resonance to me as Mr. Clean or the Maytag repairman commercials did to her. We could have been Martians to each other, for all the pop-cultural references we had in common. I found it a huge turn-on.

After a while, when we'd had enough Becherovka and it was time for Eliska to go home, I walked with her through Old Town Square, where we paused at Prague's famous fifteenth-century Astronomical Clock. We arrived just in time to hear its chimes ring and watch the ancient wind-up wooden figure of Death pop out for his top-of-the-hour dance with the Seven Deadly Sins, like Hell's own cuckoo. Some six hundred years before Walt Disney built his famous pirate ride, the Czechs already possessed the technology to make creepy wooden robots that could scare the crap out of little kids. Impressive.

After Death finished his mechanical dance and retired for another hour, I leaned in to give Eliska a kiss. I'd been thinking about doing it all night, but for some reason was having trouble plucking up my courage. Normally, I wasn't at all shy about first kisses. On the contrary, I loved the adrenaline rush of the chase, the thrill of fresh conquest; it was only later on, after I'd kissed a girl for the fourth or fifth time, as a threat of a relationship began to form, that I started getting nervous. But with Eliska, it was different. She made me feel like Fred Astaire in *Silk Stockings,* wooing comrade Cyd Charisse with his decadent capitalistic charm. As far as I was concerned, that moment in Old Town Square couldn't have been more romantic if I'd been wearing a top hat and tails and Eliska a silvery ball gown. I wanted to sweep the girl off her feet. I wanted to knock her socks off.

"What was the purpose of that?" she asked when it was over, scratch-cutting me back to reality. She didn't sound angry or even all that annoyed. She just seemed curious to hear my explanation for what she obviously considered irrational behavior. "You live thousands of miles away," she said. "You are leaving Prague tomorrow. You will never see me again. What was the point of kissing? What possible good could come of it?"

It was a good question. Sure, Eliska was beautiful, smart, and charming—that had a lot to do with why I kissed her. She also had that sexy spy girl accent that made me want to stuff her into a car trunk and smuggle her across Checkpoint Charlie. But she was right. I did live thousands of miles away. I probably wouldn't see her again. There was no point in kissing at all. It was the story of my life: the only women I ever wanted were the ones I couldn't have. Samantha. Czech translators who lived on the other side of the planet.

"Do you think I could see you again before I go?" I asked Eliska. "Would that be possible? Would you meet me for breakfast tomorrow? I have time before my flight. Maybe just a cup of coffee?"

Eliska considered the request. It seemed like she was making a big decision. "If you want," she finally said, shrugging her shoulders, "you could meet me near the Charles Bridge. I have an appointment nearby." She jotted the name of an intersection and some other numbers on a piece of scrap paper and handed it to me. "But I don't know why you would want to meet me. It makes no sense."

The next morning, before going to the airport, I did indeed stop at the intersection near the Charles Bridge. I waited fifteen minutes. Then another fifteen minutes. But Eliska never showed.

If this book were the movie constantly playing out in my head, everything at this point would get all wavy again as we dissolved out of the flashback and returned to Cambodia. DeeDee Devry has just finished making me perspire more than Richard Nixon in a Swedish sauna. I'm strolling across a pothole-filled strip of tarmac at Siem Reap Airport and boarding a tiny twenty-seat rice-paddy jumper bound for Hong Kong, where I'll have a five-hour layover before getting on a jumbo jet for the sixteen-hour flight back to America. I am at the end my grand tour.

Somewhere over Vietnam, though, my plane got struck by lightning. We'd been in the air maybe twenty minutes when the tiny cabin was suddenly flooded with a flash of blue light, followed a millisecond later by a loud popping noise. That was it. Nothing else bad happened. But because none of the flight attendants spoke English, it took a while for them to convince me it was okay to remove my head from between my knees.

When we landed at Hong Kong International, I headed right for the bar inside the first-class lounge. It was too

early in the morning for straight vodka, so I ordered a
Bloody Mary. It wasn't just the lightning bolt that had
spooked me. Getting stood up on that bridge in Prague
had rattled me, too, and that weirdness with Devry at
Angkor Wat didn't help much either. Clearly something
was wrong. My mojo was on the fritz. I needed to get it
looked at. It was turning me into a wreck.

I ordered a second Bloody Mary and turned my attention to the flat-panel video monitor hanging on a wall.
A young Asian lad of about ten had slipped away from
his parents and commandeered the remote control. He
was speed-flipping through hundreds of cable channels. I
watched as the collective cultures of a dozen civilizations
flickered across the TV. Chinese game shows, Australian
soap operas, Taiwanese dish-washing soap commercials—I got a few seconds of each as the kid raced through
the dial. And then, for an instant, an all-too-familiar face
appeared on the screen. Samantha's.

It was that home video footage of ten-year-old Sammy
wading into the ocean on Cape Cod, the same tape her
parents had given *20/20* for its interview last year. A
Hong Kong channel was using the clip, along with dozens
of others, for their own special on Mr. and Mrs. Mars.
After a brief tug-of-war with the kid over the remote, I
was able to turn up the volume and listen to the Chinese
TV hosts talk about my ex-girlfriend, even though I didn't
understand a word of their Cantonese. Mars hadn't been
doing any public appearances lately—his worsening condition made it too difficult—but even in Southeast Asia
the media continued to be fascinated by his tragic plight.
I couldn't believe it. Samantha was still haunting me from

the other side of the screen. No matter where I went, no matter how far away, I couldn't escape her.

After a couple more Bloody Marys, I realized that the gecko in my hotel room in Siem Reap had been right. It was time for me to wake up. It was beginning to dawn on me that I'd spent decades chasing after shadows on screens. I could no longer tell who was real in my life and who was a one-dimensional illusion. Seeing Sammy's face on Hong Kong TV made me see that I had romanticized her exactly the same way I idealized movie stars. I put them both atop the same pedestal—with everybody else crushed underneath. And if that was the case, what did it say about my feelings for Sam, about what our relationship had been, really? Had it honestly been love? Or was it something more akin to what a fan feels toward a distant and unattainable object of adulation?

I thought about Sammy's relationship with Johnny. I remembered her describing the grim daily routine of taking care of her husband. Helping him eat, dress, go to the bathroom—it required tireless, round-the-clock effort. I asked myself if I could do that for Samantha. Could I do it for anyone, period? I found it hard to imagine. I doubted I was capable of that kind of devotion. I couldn't even handle veiny arms. Being slightly drunk in an airport halfway around the world put things into grim perspective. No wonder my relationships were doomed to failure. At thirty-five, I hadn't grown up at all. On the contrary. I was reverting, de-maturing. I had been a far more advanced human being as an adolescent than I was as an adult. At least when I was a teen I had a girlfriend.

13

When I got back to New York, I took a long hard look at the life I'd built for myself in the city that never sleeps and decided to move to Los Angeles, the city that hits the snooze button and dozes till noon.

I pitched the move to Carla and my other bosses at *KNOW* as if I were volunteering to spy behind enemy lines. If I was ever going to truly understand the famous, I argued, I needed to live and hide among them. In truth, I just needed a change. I wanted to get away from the blare and bustle of Manhattan. Not to mention the disaster that was my social life. I'd pretty much exhausted my romantic opportunities among Robin's actress friends— "You'll never date below Fourteenth Street again," she told me—and I wasn't finding much love anywhere else in the city. Most of all, though, I was determined to get over Samantha. I had to finally accept that I was never going to get her back—Johnny's illness made it impossible—and I wanted to put some distance between us. Twenty-five hundred miles wasn't enough—I couldn't even avoid her in Hong Kong—but it would have to do.

I rented a cool, airy loft in the Venice Canals, my favorite part of LA. The canals were the brainchild of a kooky nineteenth-century tobacco mogul–turned–real estate developer named Abbot Kinney, who adored the Venice in Italy so much he decided, a hundred years ago, to re-create it on the beachfront south of Santa Monica. Even back then, Los Angeles was a mecca for lunatic dreamers. It's hard to imagine anyone ever mistaking Kinney's wacky waterway for its European inspiration, but the neighborhood still had lots of eccentric charm. The artists and photographers and film industry hipsters who were my neighbors would paddle around the canals in tiny wooden boats, feeding bread crumbs to the ducks that nested under the footbridges. At dusk, as the sun sank into the Pacific and the jasmine flowers scented the air like God's own Glade fresheners, it was as magical as any village in Tuscany.

Typical LA transplant, I blew most of my money on a car—a vintage Porsche Speedster. It had enough miles on its odometer to reach Venus, but the dual-tone black and cream leather interior had me at hello. I'd never purchased something so expensive. My hands were trembling as I signed the paperwork. When the young, shaggy-haired salesman at the specialty dealership handed me the keys, I nearly gave him a hug. Then he slipped me a CD. "It's my band," he said. "Maybe you could write about us in *KNOW?*"

This sort of thing happened a lot once I moved to LA. The Realtor who rented me my loft had written a film script—when he found out I wrote about movies for *KNOW,* he asked me to take a look. When the guy who cut my hair on Main Street in Santa Monica found out, he gave me his head shot. I thought I understood how preoccupied this city was with celebrity, but as a resident of LA, mingling with the natives, I began to see just how deep the obsession went. In New York, status was measured in square footage, with cocktail party conversations inevitably turning to real estate. Manhattan or Brooklyn? Do you own or rent? Co-op or condo? But in Los Angeles, status was calculated on a different scale. It was all about proximity to fame. If someone told you that her dermatologist's daughter once dated Scott Baio's best friend's brother—that was fungible social currency.

As a writer for *KNOW,* I wasn't able to make anybody famous. I was only able to make already-famous people slightly more famous. But my job gave me access to the overlords who did have that sort of power. One of the first things I did when I moved to LA was drive my sporty little convertible into the back lots and meet with the major studio heads. I'll never forget their gigantic, meticulously decorated offices. One looked like the wicker wing of the Getty Museum, with an enormous straw sculpture of an ancient Japanese warrior-god looming in a corner. Another had been done up to resemble a Hamptons beach house. I met with one studio head in the biggest conference room I'd ever seen, just the two of us sitting at a table so enormous you could land a Harrier jet on it. There were NO SMOKING signs all over the building, but he lit up a big fat stinky cigar anyway.

"They let you smoke in here?" I foolishly asked.

"Who are *they*?" he answered, puffing fumes in my face.

From my encounters with Hollywood's great-and-powerful Ozes, I got a fresh perspective on fame. Meeting studio chiefs and producers and other industry bigwigs was like getting a tour of Detroit by the heads of the car companies. I saw the assembly lines where celebrities were manufactured, the boardrooms where they were marketed, the showrooms where they were wheeled out to the public. I learned the vernacular of the industry ("first dollar gross," "fuckability quotient"), as well as the strange geometric theories that ruled the city (in Hollywood, the people of the world were divided into four "quadrants"—male, female, over twenty-five, and under twenty-five—with the ideal movie appealing to all of them in equal measure). To these titans of showbiz, fame was nothing more than a commodity, like lumber or steel, that generated billions of dollars a year. As one exec proudly put it during lunch in the Warner Bros. commissary, "Celebrities are America's number two export, after munitions."

I moved to Los Angeles just as the town was gearing up for the high holy days: awards season. That was an education in itself. I'd been in LA for the Oscars before, as well as the Golden Globes, but I'd never experienced the frenzy that consumes the city in the months and weeks leading to the ceremonies. I'd never seen the backstabbing politics so close up, either. Just a few weeks after I arrived in LA, in November 2005, I got a call from an "animal activist" who tried to get me to write a story about how he felt sheep and horses and other critters had been mistreated on the set of *Brokeback Mountain,* which was up for Best Picture that year. He was particularly upset that an elk had been given anesthesia during a hunting scene. Weirdly, the number that popped up on my phone's caller ID had the same first six digits as a major talent agency that happened to rep an actor in *Crash,* which was also up for Best Picture (and won).

The most astounding thing about awards season, though, was the parties. They weren't merely lavish—they were better produced than some of the films being celebrated. Many were held in old-school Hollywood hotspots like Skybar and Spago, but the most dazzling soirees took place up in the Hills, at the private residences of studio heads and super-producers. I thought movie stars lived well, but these guys had palaces that would impress an Iraqi dictator. One night, just before the 2006 Oscars, I nearly stripped the clutch on my Speedster inching uphill behind a mile-long line of cars and limos heading to the home of Jay Moses, chief of Monarch Pictures, the studio that produced the Jack Montana movies. Moses owned not one, not two, but three mansions on neighboring plots, along with two guest houses and a separate building just for his private screening room. As if that weren't space enough for the party, a giant tent had been erected on one of his lawns. Inside, I could hear Beck playing. Not on a sound system—live, onstage.

I was used to seeing celebrities up close, of course, but not casually relaxing together in such huge numbers. It reminded me of that old Bugs Bunny cartoon in which Elmer Fudd works as a waiter at the Macrumbo Room. He serves dinner to animated Humphrey Bogart and Lauren Bacall ("Baby wants rabbit . . .") while cartoon versions of Frank Sinatra and Ray Milland drink at the bar. Everywhere I turned, there were cartoony-looking movie stars. In one of Moses's living rooms, I saw Heath Ledger and Philip Seymour Hoffman amuse onlookers by pretending to arm wrestle. On line at the seafood buffet, I spotted Reese Witherspoon filling a plate with lobster tails and cocktail sauce. I saw George Clooney chatting up Charlize Theron and Terrence Howard chatting up Michelle Williams. When Nicole Kidman broke her heel on a stone path in the garden, I was there to act as history's witness. When Sean Penn couldn't find an ashtray, I was there to watch him stub out his cigarette on the bottom of his shoe.

After circling the scene a couple of times, I noticed a commotion at the screening room building. It was jammed with people, so I peeked through an open window. I saw our host, Jay Moses—one of the few men who could pull off an ascot in the twenty-first century—addressing a crowd of revelers. Then I noticed who the head of Monarch Pictures had his arm around. It was Chuck Fuse, the numbskull I interviewed in Prague back in the spring. It looked like he was going to get Johnny's old job after all. I headed to the bar inside the tent and waited for the bartender to look my way. Standing next to me, waiting as well, was a very thin man wearing a Nehru jacket. He looked familiar.

"I know you, don't I?" the man asked after studying me for a few seconds. "You interviewed me, didn't you? At my home?"

I couldn't believe I hadn't recognized him. It was Alistair Lyon. This guy was full of surprises. The star must have lost a hundred pounds since doing that Winston Churchill movie—all part of preparation for his next role, as Mahatma Gandhi in a hunger strike drama called *Fast*. Even more shocking, though, was the fact that he remembered me. Movie stars never remembered reporters. Unless, of course, they're angry at them. When it comes to negative press, celebrities have photographic memories. I tried to recall if there'd been anything in my story about Lyon that the great actor could have objected to.

"Yes, that was me," I said, bracing for the worst.

"I remember you asked me a lot of questions about being famous," Lyon said. "Did you ever figure it out? Fame, that is?"

He wasn't angry. He simply had a good memory. I tried to answer his question. I told him about the four quadrant theory and fuckability quotients and how celebrities were America's number two export. Lyon nodded politely until I was finished, but I could tell he wasn't buying it. Frankly, neither was I. I had seen the inside of the factory where celebrities were manufactured, watched them roll off the assembly lines and get packaged for the public. The mystery wasn't totally gone, but fame was definitely losing its luster. I was starting to realize that the sparkle and glitter that had so mesmerized me—that so mesmerized the whole world—turned out to be mostly marketing.

"Maybe," Lyon said, with the understated delivery only an Oscar winner could pull off, "you are not looking for answers in the right places."

Sammy didn't stop calling after I moved to Los Angeles. But thanks to the three-hour time difference, I wasn't being startled out of bed in the middle of the night anymore. Now the phone would ring at around eleven p.m.—two in the morning in New York, Samantha's bewitching hour. I got the sense that calling me was sort of like a mini vacation for her—a break from the depressing routine of caring for her husband and dealing with crazy Korean doctors and even crazier Alaskan family members. Sammy could relax and be herself and chat about nothing at all. As for me, I was more than glad to be Sam's holiday destination, her personal Ibiza. But I was also glad I was on the other side of the continent. After that near-kiss in my office, it felt a lot safer.

Johnny was continuing to decline, in sometimes startling ways. Along with weight loss, muscle atrophy, and spreading paralysis—he was finally forced to take his doctor's advice and was confined to a wheelchair—he also seemed to be aging rapidly. His hair and facial stubble had gone completely white, his skin was becoming wrinkled, and liver spots had started appearing on his hands. Inexplicably, the only part of his body that didn't seem affected by the brain cancer was Johnny's left arm, which remained nearly as beefy and powerful as ever. Johnny's Western doctors were at a loss to explain it, but his Eastern healers pointed to the healthy appendage as a sign that their medicines were working. "I don't think Johnny listens to them anymore," Sammy told me during one call. "He still takes their weird medicine and does their exercises, but it's more out of habit now. Whenever they tell him how well he's doing, he just looks at me and rolls his eyes."

Samantha wasn't the only one calling me in LA. Much to my surprise, my dad started phoning every so often.

This was a first—when I lived in New York, he always stubbornly waited for me to call. Months, if that's what it took. An even bigger surprise: he'd met a new lady friend. "We're not dating," he made sure I understood when he told me about her. "We just go to the movies sometimes, or have something to eat together." He'd met her at the gym his doctor had forced him to join after his heart attack. Her name was Madge, she was sixty-eight, and she was recuperating from a heart attack as well. They bonded over their mutual hatred of beta-blockers. It just goes to show, anything is possible.

Robin also phoned—sometimes three or four times a day. She had not been happy about my moving to LA, to put it mildly. "Why would you want to live in Los Angeles?" she had asked with a shocked stare when I broke the news to her. "It's a giant strip mall. It's got the personality of a paper napkin. You'll hate it there." Robin was no longer answering phones at *KNOW*. Her latest play, *Hamret?*, an update of *Hamlet* in which all the roles had been rewritten for *Scooby-Doo* characters, had been a huge success. The *Times* had given it a half-page rave. For Robin, New York was still a city full of hope and promise. But she was wrong about LA. I didn't hate it.

For one thing, the work environment was a lot more relaxing in Los Angeles than in Manhattan. The magazine rented a slick suite of offices in a tower in Brentwood for the six LA-based writers, although nobody actually spent time at "the bureau" except to pick up mail and steal office supplies. Unlike *KNOW*'s New York writers, who were always stabbing one another in the back competing for bylines and column inches, the scribes in LA strove to do as little as possible. There was supposed to be an LA bureau chief—D. B. Martin was the name on the door of his huge corner office—but nobody could remember ever seeing him behind his desk. The only time he surfaced was in public, accompanying a celebrity. One writer spotted him at Christian Bale's table during the Governors Ball. Another caught him courtside at a Lakers game with Dustin Hoffman. Like Colonel Kurtz, Martin had gone native. The local savages, mistaking his title for power, had adopted him almost as one of their own. He'd become a professional hanger-on. The horror. The horror.

Sure, there was a lot to dislike about LA. The traffic was maddening, the air quality sometimes bordered on sulfuric, and I was dealing on a daily basis with some of the most vicious and scurrilous liars and cheats you could find in any city on any continent—agents and publicists. On the other hand, Los Angeles was the only municipality I knew of with an economy based entirely on creativity. Like Washington, D.C., it was a one-industry town, except the industry here was dreams. That made LA a magnet for all sorts of lunatics, not just the sort trying to become movie stars. If you wanted to invent a new religion, or build cars that ran on french fry grease, or, like Abbot Kinney, build a European waterway on the beach, this city was ready to welcome you with open arms. I loved that about LA.

It was also, in its own spectacularly tacky way, a sexy city. Or at least jiggly. Strolling past the downtown-chic clothing shops on Melrose Avenue was like a trip to Hef World. The sidewalks were jammed with could-be Play-

mates in hot pants and halter tops, strutting like strip-
pers on a runway. Driving my Speedster at night along
bustling, neon-lit Sunset Strip—"the clitoris of LA," as
Robert Evans once described it, or should have—I'd find
myself looking at everything but the road. At every stop-
light, there'd be another billboard with a twenty-foot-tall
bikini-clad supermodel peddling the latest musk fragrance
or underwire bra. It's a wonder I didn't hit more lamp-
posts. As far as I could tell, the streets of LA truly were
paved with carefree sex. For some reason, though, my GPS
navigator kept taking me to Crazy Street.

"How do you feel about composting?" an incredibly
hot blonde asked me one night when I tried to chat her up
at Bar Marmont on Sunset. She was wearing puffy hippie
pants and a tight-fitting T-shirt with a vintage Mr. Bubble
ad on it, but she was sucking her cocktail through a straw
in a way that would make a porn star blush. "Because,
you know, I could never go to bed with a man who didn't
compost."

One of the reasons I wasn't doing better with dating
in LA, I figured, was that I didn't know how to dress like
a local. In New York, I wore a suit and a button-down
shirt, no tie. It was the uniform of the Manhattan media
drone, and I loved its Garanimals-like simplicity. Find
matching pants and jacket, and you were done. But in
LA, I discovered, only suits wore suits. And suits weren't
considered sexy. So I drove to Fred Segal in West Hollywood and bought two pairs of trendy Italian blue jeans
and some simple black Tom Cruise–style T-shirts. That
would be my new LA uniform. I was pretty pleased with
myself until the salesgirl rang up my purchases. My new

jeans and tees cost me $1,100. It made me reconsider composting.

As a sign of commitment to my decision to move to LA, I resolved to donate all my old New York clothing to the Salvation Army. I made a big production out of it, chucking items out of my closet onto the floor in the middle of my loft, turning all the pockets inside out in case I happened to have left $1,100 in one of them. I found only about six bucks in change, but I did dig up theater ticket stubs and nightclub matchbooks and cocktail napkins—the flotsam of my old dating life in Manhattan. I also found—surprise!—a fat joint that one of the Harold brothers had given me back in the spring, when I'd visited the Brooklyn set of *Kush Street,* their latest stoner comedy. The sibling filmmakers were famous for shooting movies while totally high, and when I met them they didn't disappoint. When they opened the door to their trailer, plumes of marijuana smoke wafted into the parking lot. Inside, the fumes were so thick I needed fog lights to find the sofa. I declined the joint they were passing around— I hardly needed it; just breathing the air made me hear sitar music—but after the interview Joey Harold insisted on slipping a souvenir cigarette into my jacket pocket. "To remember us by," he said with a phlegmy laugh. Somehow, I'd forgotten all about it.

I lit up the joint and continued sorting through my clothing. The pot certainly made the chore more interesting. I studied a piece of lint as if it contained the secrets of the universe. I examined an old penny as if it were Michelangelo's lost masterpiece, noticing for the first time how Lincoln's beard curled up at the end, like a gnome's.

Then, in the pocket of a tweed jacket, I found a scrap of paper with strange handwriting on it. The words weren't English—"Misenka" and "Saska"—and there was a line of numbers underneath that didn't make any sense. What the hell was this? I took another toke of pot and scratched my head. Somewhere in the slush of my gray matter, a synapse fired. This was the paper the Czech girl—Eliska, I remembered her name—had slipped me the night I had kissed her in Prague, now over a year ago. It was the address near the Charles Bridge where she had stood me up. And the long series of seemingly random digits— could that be a Czech phone number? Eliska's number? I took another drag and realized what I had to do.

If it was eight p.m. in LA, what time was it in the Czech Republic? I remembered that it was a six-hour time difference. That would make it two in the afternoon in Prague. I took another hit and grabbed the phone. Why did Sammy get to be my one and only phone buddy? Maybe Eliska and I could have a telephonic relationship, too. The night we spent together drinking that Sterno-based Czech aperitif and watching Death dance on the clock tower in Old Town Square—that had been the best date I'd had in years. True, the kiss hadn't been received as warmly as I'd hoped, but Eliska didn't slap me or call the cops. I was sure she'd be delighted to hear from me again. After carefully punching in the numbers, I waited as my call bounced off who knows how many communication satellites, and then heard the high-pitched purring of a European phone. I took one last hit and prepared to give Eliska the surprise of her life.

"*Prosim... kdo je tam?*" Eliska's voice sounded scratchy

and sleepy. Something was wrong. I stubbed the joint out on the bottom of my shoe, Sean Penn–style, and did some quick recalculating. To my horror, I instantly realized my mistake. It was a six-hour difference between New York and Prague; between LA and Prague, it was nine. And it wasn't earlier in the Czech Republic, it was later. I'd surprised Eliska, all right, but by calling her at five in the morning her time. "*Kdo je to?*" she repeated into her phone, growing impatient. "*Je pet rano!*" I didn't know what to say. So I hung up, slid the phone under my Crate & Barrel limited edition sofa pillow, and prayed they didn't have caller ID in Central Europe.

14

"Where the hell are all the people?" Robin wanted to know. "How come the streets are so empty? It looks like a national emergency."

We were touring LA in my Speedster on a balmy February afternoon in 2007. I drove past the mansions of Beverly Hills, slowing down to show Robin the one on Sunset with the life-size bronze statues of joggers on the front lawn. I steered into the steep, winding streets of Hollywood Hills, took in the million-dollar views for a while, then looped back down into sleepy Santa Monica, and finally followed the coastline up to Malibu. We didn't see a single pedestrian the whole time. "This city is so alien," Robin said as we sat down for lunch at Neptune's Net, a bikers' hangout on the Pacific Coast Highway that served the best fried clams west of Nantucket. "I might as well be visiting the surface of the moon. Are you going to eat that coleslaw?"

Robin wasn't in LA just to see me. Thanks to the success of her plays, she'd been approached for a job as a staff writer on *DINKs,* the hit cable-TV dramedy about four well-to-do childless couples—Dual Income No Kids—who lived in different parts of Los Angeles and came from different ethnic and generational groups, but somehow all managed to be friends. At first, Robin told her agent she wasn't interested. She was a lifelong New Yorker. There was no way she would ever leave Manhattan to write for a crappy TV show, or even a pretty good one. Then her agent told her how much the gig paid, and she was on the next flight to LA.

I, of course, was delighted at the prospect of Robin moving to Los Angeles, and invited her to camp out on my sofa while she was in town interviewing with *DINKs*'s showrunners. If she took the job, I'd have my old wingman back. With Robin's help, in no time at all I'd be sleeping with scores of pretty young actresses again. In fact, there was one in particular on *DINKs* who I was hoping to meet, a sexy redhead improbably named Purity Love. She had a small but regular part as a new mom who was always rubbing her fertility in the other characters' faces. But if Robin was to be the solution to my West Coast dating woes, I'd first have to convince her that Los Angeles wasn't the lunar surface. "LA has a very vibrant lesbian community," I told her, waving a clam for emphasis. "You've seen *The L Word.* There are cafés in this city that cater exclusively to beautiful gay girls . . ."

"Theater in LA is a joke," Robin said, ignoring me. "How could I write plays in LA? It'd be like trying to toboggan in Tahiti."

"How much do writers for *DINKs* get paid?" I asked. "What was that number again? It had so many zeros, I lost track . . ."

Robin, of course, accepted the job offer, and we agreed she would stay on my sofa in Venice until she could find an apartment of her own. It was the first time I had shared my home with a woman for longer than a one-night stand since Samantha and I lived together in Greenwich Village. I have to say, it was sort of fun, for the first week. I'd come home from a hard day interviewing celebrities and would find Robin in my kitchen, cremating vegetables in a stir-fry pan, or exploding packets of instant rice in my micro-wave. (Are all lesbians lousy cooks or was it just her?) While we picked at the charred bits of food on our plates, I tutored Robin in the vernacular she'd need to survive in her new city. "You don't leave voice mail," I explained, "you 'leave word.' And you don't play phone tag—here it's called 'trading calls.' And when you make lots of calls in a row, that's called 'rolling calls.'" Robin nodded and took mental notes.

After a couple of weeks, though, I began to wonder if Robin was ever going to leave. She'd started her new job writing for *DINKs,* had leased a gigantic SUV that she practically needed a ladder to climb into, but seemed to have made no progress at all in finding a place to live. Every once in a while, she'd inquire about a neighborhood. "How about Marina del Rey?" she'd ask. "Flight atten-dants and swingers," I'd answered. "Hollywood Hills?" "Agents and other douchebags." But there was no serious apartment hunt going on. And I was beginning to want my space back. It was driving me nuts that Robin would take at least two hours in my bathroom every morning. It was somehow extra exasperating that she would always emerge looking exactly the way she did when she went in.

And then I came home from work one day and Robin
announced that she had found true love on the set of
DINKs. With an actress named Purity Love. "Wait a sec—
she's gay?" I asked, stunned. "Gayer than Peppermint
Patty at an Indigo Girls concert," Robin chirped, dancing around my kitchen as she smelted a pot of angel hair
pasta into sludge. "We're going on a date on Saturday. *She*
asked *me* out. Can you believe it? I'm really starting to
like LA."

I congratulated her on her new romance. If anyone
deserved a little Love, it was Robin. Her dating life was
almost as calamitous as my own, although her trouble
was of a different sort. She fell in love too easily, then
would inevitably get her heart smashed to bits. I'd nursed
her through at least a dozen traumatic breakups. I was
beginning to worry that Robin was losing hope. I was also
worrying that Purity Love could do some serious damage
if things didn't work out. I didn't say anything out loud,
but I had some niggling suspicions.

Purity was not hugely famous. *DINKs,* in fact, was her
first break, or at least her first since she was seventeen.
Her only other credit on IMDb was in 1997, when she
starred with three other teenagers in a Nickelodeon kid-
die program called *Boogie Girls*. The reasons for Love's
abrupt departure from that show were cloudy—she either
walked away in a huff or was fired—but one day thousands of toddlers turned on their TVs and saw a different
redhead singing and dancing about sharing toys and making friends. Children's television could be such a jungle.
Now that she had bounced back with *DINKs,* though, I'd
been seeing Love's picture in the party pages of LA's local

glossy magazines, always in a slinky, low-cut dress, and with her arm around some up-and-coming actor or hot young director. Exclusively of the male variety.

At least Robin's love affair kept her out of my hair for the next couple of weeks. I could finally go to the bathroom in the morning again. She was out all night almost every night. Every couple of days Robin would come whirling back into the loft to collect some personal items, then rush off again. Sometimes she'd even have a minute for a quick conversation.

"How are things going with your new girlfriend?" I asked, watching Robin dig into my clothes dryer looking for clean underwear.

"It's terrifying," she said, laughing. "I really think she's the one, Max, I really do. I'm so in love with this girl it's disgusting. She's unlike anyone I've ever been with . . ." She found a pair of freshly washed panties and looked up from the dryer. "But that's what's terrifying. What if it doesn't work out? I don't know if I could take that."

"But what if it does?" I said. I'd been a little jealous of Robin, and I still had my suspicions about Purity, but I had to root for their love affair. I'd never seen Robin so happy. It was like a light had been switched on behind her eyes. I hadn't yet met Purr, as Robin called her, but I was grateful to Love for what she was doing to my friend. I only wished I had somebody to do the same to me.

The phone rang at a quarter past eleven. I had a pretty good hunch who was calling. Where she was, it was a quarter past two.

"We're at Mount Sinai," Samantha said between sobs. "Johnny's in the emergency room. All of a sudden he started having convulsions and couldn't breathe. The doctors don't know what's going on. It's terrible, Max. I think he's dying."

I caught the next plane to New York. It was an impulsive thing to do—if Robin had been on my sofa that night, she would have talked me out of it—but after Samantha hung up the phone to get back to her convulsing husband, all I could hear were her sobs. It cost seventy-five thousand frequent flyer miles—the only seat available on the last flight out of LA was in first class—but I didn't care. When it came to rushing to Sammy's side in her hour of need, I would pay any price.

No, I most certainly was not hoping for Johnny's death. That would have made me a monster. Truthfully, as I flew to New York, I was crossing every finger that Mars would be okay. Not just for his sake, but for Sammy's. I hated the idea of her suffering any sort of pain. But I'd be lying if I didn't admit that in the lizard part of my brain, where evil thoughts slither and hiss, I did wonder what would happen if Mars happened to die. I know, it's terrible, but I couldn't help myself. I imagined soothing Samantha through her grief. Growing close with her again. And then, after an appropriate mourning period had passed, taking her back into my arms as the One once again. God, I hated myself.

When the plane landed at JFK at 10:30 a.m., I grabbed my overhead bag and headed for the taxi stand. I hadn't called ahead for car service, or a hotel room, for that matter. I hadn't even told Sammy I was coming. I didn't want her to try to dissuade me. As I waited for a cab to take me to Mount Sinai Hospital, I took out my cell phone to call *KNOW*'s travel department. They'd be able to arrange a room for me somewhere. I noticed I had a voice mail. "Hey Max, it's Sammy. Everything is okay. Whew. Johnny is breathing normally and the convulsions have stopped. They're going to release him later today. They think it was a reaction to one of the drugs the Koreans gave him. Jesus, was that scary! Anyway, thanks for taking my panic-stricken call last night and for being so sweet about it. You're a great friend . . ."

Of course, I was glad that Johnny was okay—but I felt like an idiot. I really was pathetic. I had flown across the country in the middle of the night just because a girl I once lived with was worried about her husband's health. Clearly I had made no progress whatsoever. No matter how many miles I put between us, no matter the hours I spent up in the air, no matter how many other perfectly wonderful women I met—I thought of the one who left me hanging on the Charles Bridge in Prague— I always ended up boomeranging back to Samantha. What we had was not a normal, healthy relationship between a grown-up man and a grown-up woman. It was more like the relationship between a grown-up dog and his grown-up mistress. When she whistled, I came running. Why? It was like I was stuck in my own private sitcom hell, forever doomed to make the same jackass mistake over and over again. Now I knew how Gilligan felt. I wasn't ever going to get off this stupid island.

I did an about-face and walked back into JFK airport to catch the next flight to LA. Six hours later, when I stepped through the front door of my loft, I was so exhausted and relieved to be home I almost didn't notice Robin weeping on my sofa. I tossed my bag into a corner—there really wasn't any need to tell her about Sammy's call and how it sent me scurrying to New York—and sat down beside her. "What's going on?" I asked in a whisper. "What happened?"

"Purity is a bitch!" Robin howled. "She's a deceitful, conniving, cold-blooded bitch."

"Oh c'mon, it can't be that bad. What happened?" I was praying it was just a lovers' spat, something easily repairable.

"She told me that if I didn't write more lines for her character, she was going to break up with me," Robin explained between sobs. "She said if I really cared about her, I should prove it by making her a star. That's the only reason she went out with me in the first place—to get more lines! I found out from one of the producers that she does this all the time. Whenever they hire new writers, she throws herself at them. Male, female, whatever, she doesn't care, so long as she thinks they can help her career . . ."

"Wait a second," I interrupted. "I want to make sure I understand this correctly. She's sleeping with the *writers* to get ahead? How stupid is this girl?"

"Yeah, right?" Robin agreed, laughing through her tears.

An idea popped into my head as I brewed my friend a cup of tea. My own love life was still a disaster-in-progress, but that didn't mean Robin's had to be. Maybe there was a way I could help give her some closure, help heal her wounded heart. "Robin," I said over the kettle whistle, "how would you feel about revenge?"

Part one of my plan was to get my editor, Carla, to agree to a story on DINKs. I gave her a spiel about how the show pointed to the changing definition of the American family in pop culture. How it spoke to a long-overlooked but growing demographic—married people who don't reproduce.

"I already assigned a DINKs story to Cartwright," Carla said. "But if he's willing to give it up, it's all yours."

Justin Cartwright was one of the other writers in the Los Angeles bureau. Normally his beat was sports, but he'd occasionally dive into a TV piece. "Oh, yeah, dude, that would be great!" Cartwright said when I offered to pick up his DINKs story. "I'm scheduled to go on the set next week, but there's a Segway race in Long Beach that I'm dying to sign up for . . ."

DINKs was shot on a pair of soundstages in Culver City. Four different living rooms, assorted bedrooms, kitchens, and dining rooms were in one building; all the other sets, including the bank where one character worked as a teller and the emergency room where another was a nurse, were in the other. The producers and writers, Robin included, had their offices in bungalows on the other side of the lot. The economy and efficiency of TV production always impressed me, especially after spending so much time on feature films, where sets were so often built to be blown up.

I interviewed each of the main actors in their trailers,

which were parked next to the soundstages. First, Monica Sellers, the fifty-eight-year-old ex–soap star who played the ER nurse, then Elmo Barker, the thirty-two-year-old African American stand-up comic who played the bank teller, followed by Jessica Mildred, the twenty-eight-year-old Australian actress who played the childless wife of a rising young politician. All this, though, was merely foreplay. The real screwing was coming up.

Purity Love didn't have a big enough part to warrant a trailer of her own—as a second-tier character, she was in a scene only every couple of episodes—so we conducted our interview in one of the bedroom sets. We'd never met, so she didn't know my face, but I was concerned she might recognize my name. Robin had undoubtedly mentioned me once or twice. I needn't have worried. When she saw me getting a cup of coffee at the catering tables, she headed right over. "You're Justin Cartwright, the writer from *KNOW*, aren't you?" she said, shaking my hand like we were already best friends. Publicists usually send out memos to cast and crew when a journalist is visiting the set. Purity had obviously read an outdated one and had been studying to butter up the wrong journalist. "I really loved your piece last week on professional volleyball . . ."

This was working out even better than I could have planned. For the next hour, I let Love think I was Justin Cartwright. And Justin, that shameless suck-up, lit a bonfire under Purity's ego. I told her she was the best part of *DINKs*, that her nimble comic timing and soaring dramatic abilities were being woefully underutilized by the show's writers and producers—an injustice I promised to point out in my article. Purity was so thrilled she was literally bouncing on the bed. "You know, Justin," she said, putting a hand on my knee, "we should really hang out together sometime. When neither of us is working."

"Oh, I'd like that very much, Purity," I said.

"Call me Purr," she said, with a flirty smile.

The following week, when my piece on *DINKs* was published, I got revenge not only for Robin but for all the other writers Love had screwed over in her lust for more screen time. I did the absolute worst thing a journalist could do to an actress. I left her out of the article. Completely. I didn't mention her name once. According to Robin, Love flew into a rage when she read it, ripping the magazine into pieces and storming off the set. She created such a commotion, kicking one of the key grips in the shin as she exited, that the producers were considering getting rid of her. Another redheaded actress could easily replace her.

Now I knew what it felt like to use my journalistic powers for good rather than evil. Seeing the laughter in Robin's eyes as she told me the whole story, I felt better than I had in months. For once in my life, I was the super-hero.

15

"Pack your Bermuda shorts, Max. You're going to the Bahamas!"

Carla, my editor, was on the other end of the line. She'd dialed my number at the office in Brentwood, but I had that line pretty much on permanent call forwarding. I hadn't stepped foot in the bureau in weeks. When Carla called to tell me she was sending me to the set of the next Jack Montana movie—the first *not* to star Johnny Mars—I was at home in Venice, lounging on my sofa, watching *La Dolce Vita* on cable with a big bag of cheese puffs propped on my stomach. Max in his resting state.

"You want *me* to write about the new Jack Montana movie?" I whined into the phone. "Carla, are you sure that's such a great idea?"

"Max, you're the world's leading expert on Montana movies," she said. "You can recite the titles in reverse-chronological order. Plus, you've already interviewed Chuck Fuse. He knows you. It'll make for a better interview."

"I don't know, Carla. It's not like he's going to remember me . . ."

"Max," she said, growing impatient, "I'm sending you to the Bahamas. Bring me a snow globe."

I had nothing against the Bahamas. I was sure it was a very nice place. But I was starting to find visiting movie sets, even the ones in LA, more and more of a drag. I'd been to so many that they started to blend together. I had recently interviewed Jennifer Aniston, but whether it was on the set of *Rumor Has It . . .* or *The Break-Up* I couldn't for the life of me remember. What's more, I didn't care. I found myself not only losing interest in my job, but, for the first time in my life, in the whole of pop culture. I guess you could say I was suffering from post-dramatic set-visit syndrome.

Even if I wasn't in the midst of a career crisis, though, visiting a Jack Montana production was pretty much the last thing I wanted to do. Just thinking about it made my stomach queasy. Johnny had made several more trips to the ER for convulsions and, on one terrible night, a bout of temporary blindness—Sammy kept me up to date with real-time reports on every emergency. It wasn't logical—I doubted I could explain it to Carla—but traveling to a Jack Montana set to interview the guy who was replacing Johnny felt somehow wrong, like a betrayal. The poor man wasn't even dead yet.

Also, to be frank, the new Montana movie sounded terrible. I even hated its cutesy title—*Less Talk, More Killing*. Where was the traditional nod to American history that made *Rocket's Red Glare* and *Give Me Death* such iconic movie names? For another thing, the director hired to reboot the franchise in the post-Mars era was Gary 7even, the pompous hack and shameless self-promoter (his real name, before he started adding numerals to it, was Gary Sevetini) who started his filmmaking career by turning the Jimmy Stewart classic *Harvey* into *Bad Rabbit,* a shocking splatter flick about a six-foot killer bunny. I'd read an interview in which 7even said that Special Agent Montana would no longer deliver witty one-liners after blowing away bad guys. In fact, in 7even's film, Montana would barely speak at all. "My dream," the director said, "would be to make a totally silent Jack Montana movie."

3at me, 7even.

My biggest problem with the movie, though, was Chuck Fuse. I just couldn't see him playing my childhood hero, or anybody's childhood hero. I didn't care how many street luge championships he'd won at the X Games, he wasn't a movie star. He was too goofy looking, for one thing, with that huge, ludicrous pompador and teeny ears and beady eyes. And while his voice was deep enough, he had a pothead drawl that made everything he said sound 50 percent stupider. The film I'd watched him shoot in Prague, *Boom!,* had done okay when it was released in the summer of 2006, earning $150 million domestic, but Fuse couldn't take all the credit for that. The pyrotechnics were the real star of that picture. Of course, I knew that Johnny Mars had once been a young, untested actor, before being cast as Jack Montana. But I was twelve years old at the time. It wasn't as big an issue to me back then.

Anyway, in the fall of 2007, I flew to Paradise Island, the sun-dappled Bahamian atoll where production was about to begin on the new Montana movie. Most of the film's crew was staying at the Poseidon, a gigantic, crowded, Vegas-style family resort where vacationers splashed on waterslides and bodysurfed on artificial waves in giant pools. But the stars of the movie—as well as visiting journalists from important magazines—were housed down the road, at the ultra-exclusive, super-secluded Surfside Club. Once the grandest rubber plantation in the Bahamas, the property had been purchased and renovated by a Dutch travel conglomerate, and was now the Caribbean's poshest playground for people with too much disposable income. The luxurious beachfront chalets, where Fuse and 7even were staying, rented for $20,000 a night. I ended up in Surfside's slums, a $600-a-night room in "the Big House," the giant colonial pile where the slaves slept back when the place was still a rubber tree farm. Of course, improvements had been made since then; I had a king-size featherbed, a Jacuzzi tub in the bathroom, and French doors leading to a balcony overlooking a stunning tropical garden.

On my first evening in the Bahamas, there was a pool party at the Surfside celebrating the film's start of production. Fuse and 7even were the hosts. I opened my suitcase and dug around for the white Sonny Crockett–style linen suit I'd purchased just for the trip. It was wrinkled beyond recognition, so I tried that old traveler's trick of hanging it in the bathroom while running steaming hot water in the shower. When I put the suit on, I looked like I'd been through a car wash without a car. I wore it to the party anyway.

There was a calypso band playing Jack Montana theme music, a giant ice sculpture of the special agent's famous .45 Magnum (after fifteen minutes in the tropical heat, it looked like a derringer), and a huge blown-up reproduction of the ad in *Variety* announcing Fuse's casting. "CHUCK FUSE *IS* JACK MONTANA," it said in block letters over a photo of the actor's grinning face. I still wasn't buying it, but I had to concede, grudgingly, that it was a nice party. The crew was just getting to know one another, so it was easy to mingle and be sociable. Even 7even was on his best behavior, chatting with assistants and introducing the grips to "Montana Girls," the models-slash-extras who were always strewn about scenes in Montana movies like so much set dressing. In a matter of hours, virtually everyone at the party would hate 7even's guts, and with good reason. His tyrannical, idiosyncratic directing style would make Lars von Trier burst into tears. But right now, the night before the first day of shooting, there was nothing but love in the air.

I was sipping a Bahama Mama cocktail, engrossed in my own conversation with a Montana Girl named Shirley, when I spotted Chuck Fuse out of the corner of my eye. He had taken a seat at a table next to the shallow end of the pool, joining a half dozen other partiers who were digging into baked crab and grilled rock lobster. I recognized the person to his left. It was hard not to. John Goodman was playing the supervillain in the film. But I couldn't quite make out the face of the woman to Fuse's right. There were too many people blocking my line of sight. Even so, I could tell she was a knockout. I definitely needed a better look. Only half paying attention to what Shirley was saying, I jockeyed around for a better angle. Jesus, she *was* gorgeous. The last time I'd seen cheekbones like those was when I met Eliska in Prague. And then my jaw dropped.

It *was* Eliska.

What the hell was she doing in the Bahamas? I couldn't figure it out. But then it all became hideously clear. My heart sank as Fuse wrapped his beefed-up arms around Eliska, gave her an affectionate squeeze, and planted a big kiss on her cheek. Obviously, she was his girlfriend. They must have hooked up on *Boom!* and been dating ever since. Somehow their romance had slipped under the tabloids' radar—Fuse was pretty good at keeping his private life private—but there was no mistaking what was going on between them at this party. Gossip columnists call it "canoodling."

What the fuck? Why were movie stars always stealing my girlfriends? Okay, so my relationship with Eliska consisted of one kiss and a botched long-distance phone call, but *theoretically* she *could* have been my girlfriend, in a different reality. She'd been the first woman I'd met since Sammy who actually got under my skin, in a good way. I knew, of course, that one of the things contributing to my attraction was the fact that she lived seven time zones away, on the other side of the planet: I always wanted what I couldn't have. Still, there was something different about this girl. For some reason, just thinking about her made me smile. But once again a movie god had swooped down from Mount Famous and snatched a woman away from me. I ducked out of the party before Eliska saw me.

As I lay in my feather bed in the Big House listening to a tropical symphony of insect-chirping in the garden below my windows, I asked myself why I was always falling for unattainable women. Was it intentional? Was I deliberately choosing impossible mates as a way to protect myself from intimacy and relationships? Well, duh, of course I was. But that didn't mean my feelings for Eliska weren't true. She was the first girl in ages to make my heart pound outside my chest like Pepé Le Pew's. That was real. That was genuine. I wasn't making that up. It wasn't my fault she was unattainable.

The first shot of the day was, naturally, an action sequence. Jack Montana jumps on a motorcycle and races through the streets of Nassau while being chased by a bad guy in a Lamborghini tricked out with machine guns and missile launchers. At the end of the scene, after Montana outmaneuvers the Lamborghini—it smashes into a banana truck and blows up—Montana's motorcycle screeches to a stop in front of the smoldering wreckage. He turns to an astonished innocent bystander and Fuse delivers his only dialogue of the day: "Relax, it was a rental."

The studio had insisted that 7even put the one-liners back into the script, but otherwise the director was actually coming close to fulfilling his promise of making a silent Montana picture. Aside from this and a few other chestnuts, Fuse barely had a speaking part—mostly he just grunted and growled. The ex–X Gamer wouldn't be doing much of his own action, either; the studio had been quite firm about that. Stunt doubles would take all the risks. All Chuck had to do was show up in costume at the end of a scene, switch places with the stuntman, and deliver a killer quip for the close-up. For this he was being paid $7 million.

I turned up at the set—an abandoned concrete factory in Coral Harbour—at nine in the morning and watched as a special effects crew rigged the banana truck with detonators. Fuse and 7even were in their air-conditioned trailers while the rest of the crew were keeping cool in other ways—fanning themselves with script pages under palm trees, lying down on benches in the catering tent— waiting for the explosion to be ready. I didn't think Eliska would be there. As the star's girlfriend, she'd more likely be lounging on one of Surfside's private beaches or shopping at one of its overpriced boutiques. But there she was, sitting in the shade under a palm tree, reading a book.

I hesitated. Was it still proper for me approach her? Now that she was a star's special friend and not a crew member, would I be crossing a social barrier? Did I need to ask the unit publicist's permission? Screw it, I decided, and walked over to say hello. As I got closer, I zoomed in on the thick book she was reading. It took a second to decipher the Czech, but it was Michel Foucault's *The History of Sexuality*. I wracked my brain for a Foucault reference but my knowledge of twentieth-century French post-structuralism was a bit rusty.

"They were all out of Hannah Arendt at the bookstore?" was the best I could come up with.

"It's you!" Eliska said, jumping up. "I heard a writer from *KNOW* was coming to interview Chuck. I was wondering if it would be you."

"You know, I happen to be an expert on Foucault's theories on sexuality . . ."

"Oh, I bet you are," she said, laughing. Her spy girl accent was even hotter than I remembered. "It's for school," she said, showing me the scribbled notes in the book's margins. "You know, I owe you an apology."

"You do?"

"Yes, I upstood you at the Charles Bridge. Upstood, no? Is that not correct? I got called in early for work that morning and had no way to reach you. I didn't have your number. I felt very bad about it."

"It's 'stood up' and it's perfectly okay," I said. "I totally understand."

"Didn't I give you my number in Prague?" she asked. "I remember writing it down."

"No, I don't think so," I said, in case she suspected me for that five a.m. hang up. "But you and Chuck—what a surprise! It seems like things are really working out for you two. I'm glad for you, I really am."

"Oh yes," she said, "Chuck is a great opportunity. He's been so generous to me. After this movie, I'll have enough money to pay all my graduate school bills. I owe him so much."

"Wait a second, he pays you?" I asked, trying to hide my shock. I knew movie stars sometimes kept mistresses on the payroll, but I couldn't believe how blasé Eliska was being about it. She didn't seem the slightest bit embarrassed or ashamed that she was being paid to be Fuse's girlfriend. I'd heard Europeans were more sophisticated about this sort of thing, but this was ridiculous.

"Of course he pays me!" Eliska said. "I'm sure some

girls would do it just for the traveling—I mean, I never thought I'd get to the Bahamas in my life!—but I'm not doing this for fun. I need the money for school."

"Well," I said, scratching my head, "I'm sure you're really great at it."

"Well, it's not hard to make Chuck happy," Eliska said. "Once you learn how he likes things, he's very easy man to please."

Before I could think of a response to that, the assistant director announced over a megaphone that they were ready to shoot the scene. At one end of the set, a brand-new Lamborghini Gallardo purred in neutral while its stunt driver waited for a signal. It was a $175,000 high-performance vehicle; in a few minutes, it'd be fricassee. At the other end of the set, techies made final checks on the banana truck. Finally, after about twenty minutes of suspense, 7even emerged from his trailer to execute his creative vision. He was wearing a white linen suit exactly like mine, only his didn't have a single wrinkle. Maybe if you have enough money there's no such thing as wrinkles. He was also wearing a fedora and had a monocle on a chain around his neck.

7even looked at the Lamborghini, then looked at the truck, then back at the Lamborghini. "It's yellow," he said, correctly identifying the color of the race car he was about to destroy. "It's fucking yellow! Who's the fucking moron who decided to put a fucking *yellow* Lamborghini in my film? It's right there in the fucking script—it's supposed to be a *red* Lamborghini! Can't you fucking idiots read!" He stormed back into his trailer and slammed the door.

For a moment, the entire crew stood frozen in silence.

You could see it in their faces—the sudden realization that the next three months of their lives were going to suck. The assistant director got back on the megaphone and postponed the sequence. Then he got on his cell phone and called the second-unit film crews that were shooting other parts of the car chase on other parts of the island with matching yellow Lamborghinis. To save time, that's how chase sequences were made—later on, all the footage from the different units would be edited together into a single seamless scene. Only now all the crews would have to stop and wait until a new fleet of red Lamborghinis could be found to replace the yellow ones. It could set the production back a week—and this was just the first day of filming.

I looked around for Eliska, but there was no sign of her. I couldn't figure it out. I didn't know her well, obviously, but from what I did know she seemed like the last woman on the planet who'd be interested in Chuck Fuse, or even in Chuck Fuse's money. The girl I kissed in Prague, she didn't care about fame. The only celebrities she was interested in had names like Spinoza and Heidegger. She was sincere. She was authentic. She was a philosophy major! How could she be with a Hollywood numbskull like Fuse? It didn't make any sense.

My interview with Fuse was the next day. It did not go well, although he couldn't have been more charming, in his big, dumb, stoner way. He even remembered me—or pretended to—from our interview in Prague. "Dude! How ya been!" he said, greeting me at the door of his

$20,000-a-night beach chalet. The place truly was spectacular, maybe even worth the price tag. I noticed a remote on the sleek glass coffee table with only one button on it. Fuse pushed it and we watched together as the living room ceiling rolled open to the sky. "Pretty freakin' cool, right?" Fuse said, handing the control to me to play with.

I kept looking for clues as to what Eliska saw in him. He did have a sort of Neanderthal charisma, I had to give him that. And I was happy to see that he had learned a touch of humility since our encounter in Prague, when he told me he was born to be a movie star. "These are very big shoes you're stepping into," I started the interview. "Johnny Mars turned the character into a cultural institution. It's hard to imagine a Jack Montana movie without him. Maybe the character should have been retired, at least for a while, out of respect for Mars . . ."

"Dude, I agree, there's no way I'm going to fill Johnny's shoes," Fuse said. "My Jack Montana is never going to be as good as Johnny's. He *invented* the character. Nobody will ever do it as well as he did. All I can do is the best I can do. And hope that I don't look like a jackass on the screen."

"How are you getting along with your director?" I continued to probe. "He seems a tad temperamental . . ."

"Gary? He's a pussycat," Fuse parried. "He just wants what he wants, and I respect that. I mean, dude, the guy is brilliant, right? Have you watched *Bad Rabbit*? Scariest freakin' film I've ever seen. That's the work of an evil genius."

Eventually, I decided to dive right into it and ask him about Eliska, albeit slightly indirectly. "I hear you had a little romance in Prague while shooting *Boom!* I know you don't like to talk about your private life, but . . ."

"What are you talking about?" Fuse interrupted. He looked surprised, and concerned. His pompadour bristled like fur on a frightened cat. "Who told you that? What have you heard?"

I wanted to keep prying, but I didn't want to get Eliska in trouble, so I moved on. But Fuse spent the rest of the interview eyeing me suspiciously. I didn't get much from him after that. I turned off the voice recorder after only about thirty minutes. Carla was going to be pissed. I really would have to bring her back a snow globe this time.

As I was walking along the beach path toward my room in Surfside's low-rent district, thinking about how uptight Fuse had become when I mentioned his personal life, I ran smack into Eliska. She was heading toward Fuse's chalet carrying a big bundle of garment bags—his wardrobe from the costume department. "How'd your interview go?" she asked brightly.

"Oh, I don't think your boyfriend likes me very much," I told her. "And I can't believe he makes you lug his laundry around for him. Here, let me help with that . . ."

Eliska pulled back and shot me a look. "My boyfriend? What are you talking about?"

"He's not your boyfriend?"

"No," she said. "Of course not."

"But I saw him hugging you at the pool party. I saw him kiss you . . ."

She laughed so hard she dropped some of the bags. "I'm his assistant!" she said. "I *work* for him. He hired me after *Boom!* wrapped. You thought I was his girlfriend? I'm not his type at all." She laughed some more as I helped her pick up the bags. "Chuck is not into girls."

"He's gay?" I asked, stunned. I really needed to get my gaydar checked.

"Wait—I didn't say that," Eliska said, suddenly remembering I was a reporter. "You can't write that. Please! It would not be right of you to write that. This is why they tell us not to talk to journalists!" She grabbed the garment bags from me, clutching them close to her chest. "Ugh," she said. "I have a mouth like the Grand Canyon."

"No, Eliska, relax, I'm not going to write about it," I assured her. "I don't care if he's gay or not. I don't write those sorts of stories, honestly I don't."

"You promise?" Eliska asked, calming down.

"Cross my heart," I said.

I was telling the truth. I normally didn't write about the sexual orientations of the people I interviewed—frankly, there are enough closeted action stars in Hollywood to mount a production of *The Pajama Game*. But I was relieved to have gotten to the bottom of the mystery. And I actually liked Fuse a lot more now that I knew he played for the other team. Suddenly all that X Games bravado and surfer-boy slang—all those "dudes" and "freakins" he slipped into every sentence—seemed sweetly endearing. The guy was obviously a much better actor than I'd been giving him credit for. Maybe he was perfect for the part, after all. Best of all, though, it meant he wasn't canoodling with Eliska.

"Do you bring a bathing suit?" Eliska asked me.

"Pardon?"

"A bathing suit—do you have one?"

"Sure, why?" I asked.

"Put it on and meet me here in an hour. I want to show you something. Something that will amaze you. It will make up for when I upstood you in Prague."

I changed into swimming trunks and a T-shirt, brushed my teeth, combed my hair, slapped on some aftershave, looked at myself in the bathroom mirror, and tried on a different T-shirt. I couldn't believe it. I was actually nervous before going on a date. I barely recognized myself.

Eliska was waiting for me on the beach. She was wearing a red one-piece swimsuit, a straw sunhat, and a pair of unlaced black Keds. On her, the outfit made my pulse do the cha-cha. "Come on," she said, leading me along the shore. "You aren't going to believe what I'm going to show you. I found it the other day. It's amazing." Wherever Eliska was taking me, it wasn't nearby. We hiked along the shore for about twenty minutes, chatting and getting reacquainted. Eventually, I got around to asking her the obvious question.

"How come you don't have a boyfriend?"

Eliska sighed. "There was a boyfriend," she answered as we walked in the sand. "He was English. His name was Jeffrey . . ."

She met Jeffrey in Prague at an art show at the old Stalin Monument in 2001, when she was twenty-three, and was immediately infatuated. He was British. He was handsome. He was an aristo. He opened doors and showed Eliska a world she hadn't even imagined existed. "I felt so backward compared to him," Eliska said. "He came from this wealthy English family and I was just this girl from nowhere." Jeffrey took the girl from nowhere for trips to France and Spain and Italy and introduced her to a stream of exciting new friends who discussed film and music and art. "I fell for him completely," Eliska said. "I was sure he was the man of my dreams." But after a year of romantic globe-trotting, Jeffrey's father back in Mayfair began tapping on his watch and telling him to come home. Youthful infatuation was one thing, but he wanted his son to marry a proper English girl, not some Slav from a former Soviet puppet state. He threatened to pull the purse strings shut if Jeffrey didn't leave Prague, and without the Slav. Jeffrey obeyed. Eliska never heard from him again.

I was so wrapped up in her sad tale that I stopped wondering where Eliska was taking me. I had found a kindred spirit. True, the details of our sob stories were different—her heart was broken because of a snobby dad out of a Merchant Ivory movie; mine because a movie star seduced my girlfriend—but we had been on the same emotional journey. We had both lost loves to worlds where we didn't belong, where we could never be more than sightseers. I wanted to tell her I knew how she felt, share my own sorrows with her. But we came to a small rocky cliff that jutted into the water, blocking the shoreline, and Eliska started climbing. "It's just over these boulders," she promised, offering her hand to help me climb.

On the other side, shielded by sand dunes, was the secluded cove Eliska had been looking for. She kicked off her sneakers and led me into the warm crystal blue sea. I gave her a quizzical glance as we waded up to our knees.

"Be patient," she said softly. "It'll be worth it, I promise."

She was still holding my hand, so I gently drew her toward me and leaned in for a kiss.

"That was nice, Max," she said when it was over. "But it still makes no sense. I'm still going to Prague when this movie is done—I have graduate school. And you're still going back to America. Besides, kissing is not why I brought you here."

Looking around, the reason Eliska brought me to this place became breathtakingly clear. All at once, we were surrounded by hundreds and hundreds of tropical fish, a wiggling swarm of brilliant fluorescent blues and reds and greens and yellows. They swam around our legs and planted ticklish kisses on our feet. "Can you believe it?" Eliska whispered, dipping a hand in the surf so that a tiny orange fish could nibble at her fingertips. "Have you ever seen anything so beautiful in your life?"

No, I surely hadn't. Watching Eliska splash in the surf, playing a gentle game of tag with her new fish friends, I had the oddest sensation. I couldn't quite put my finger on it, although I knew I'd experienced before. Ah yes, I finally remembered. This was what happiness felt like.

16

About four months after my trip to the Bahamas, Sammy called. "I'm coming to Los Angeles," she said. "Let's have dinner."

I'd been dreading hearing Sammy say those words, but it was only a matter of time. Three years had passed since that night in my office in New York when I almost kissed her. I'd flown around the world. I'd moved clear across the continent. I'd bought a sports car and a new wardrobe. So much had changed, but seeing her again, in the flesh, there was no telling what I might do.

Just thinking about it made me feel guilty, and not only because I was having impure thoughts about a married woman whose husband was in a wheelchair. I also felt like I was cheating on Eliska, which made no sense at all since I wasn't in a relationship with Eliska, not a physical one, at any rate. After our kiss in that Bahamian cove, we went our separate ways. But we exchanged e-mail addresses, and much to my surprise, I found myself involved in a regular correspondence with a new pen pal in Prague. Opening my laptop and discovering an e-mail from the Czech Republic was fast becoming a favorite part of my week.

As epistolary romances go, it wasn't exactly Lord Byron's letters to his mistress. Mostly our e-mails were simple scribbles about nothing at all, little blips of personal minutiae—movies we both liked, songs we both hated, that sort of thing—but Eliska had a way of making even these small exchanges charming. Her e-mails always struck just the right note of cautious, getting-to-know-you intimacy, and they always made me want to learn more about her. I found out, for instance, that she spoke four languages, enjoyed David Lynch films, grew up with a dog named Barah, once dreamed of becoming an ice skater, and had a habit of ending her e-mails with complicated emoticons that would take me half an afternoon to decipher. I couldn't really say what exactly I hoped to gain from our e-mail friendship—Eliska still lived seven thousand miles away—except it ended up being the closest thing to a genuine human exchange I'd had with a girl in ages.

Sammy and I met for dinner in Beverly Hills at the ludicrously trendy Shui Hotel, where she was being put up by Monarch Pictures. The studio had flown her out to talk about Johnny doing audio commentary on the DVDs of all the old Montana movies, which were being repackaged as part of the hype campaign leading up to the summer release of *Less Talk, More Killing*. Johnny had agreed to do it—he could use the quarter-million-dollar fee—but the studio was beginning to wonder if he was physically capable. A paparazzi shot had recently been published in one of the supermarket tabs—a photographer had bribed his way into Johnny's apartment building's garage and snapped a close-up of the star in his chair being loaded into a van. Johnny looked like the Crypt Keeper's handsomer twin. Sammy's mission in LA was to convince the suits that her husband would be able to perform.

I knew the Shui well. I'd stayed there myself before I moved out west, when the Four Seasons and Chateau Marmont were full up. The rooms all had instructions pretentiously stenciled on the walls: The word DREAM was printed over the bed, EAT was over the minibar. I always thought they missed an opportunity by not stenciling the bathrooms. The best part, though, was the reception desk. Behind it, built into the wall, was a big glass booth where you could observe a real-life model sleeping on a mattress in her underwear. Or his underwear, depending on whose shift it was when you checked in. I would always wonder what the conversation sounded like when the models called home—"Hey, Mom, I finally got a job in showbiz!"

The Shui had a world-class restaurant, Opium, a big airy brasserie with polished blond wood floors and impeccably white walls. It served the finest French-Chinese fusion food in LA. Or maybe it was Japanese-Cuban. Or German-Inuit. I could never remember. Whatever was on the menu, eating at the hotel made a lot of sense for Sammy. There's no way she could have slipped past the ring of paparazzi that were on permanent stakeout around the Shui. I spotted one of them smoking a cigarette on the sidewalk by the garage entrance, his camera discreetly slung behind his back. Another was leaning against a parked Jaguar, a trilby hat tipped over his brow. In New York, the paparazzi were a big, noisy marching band—you could see them coming a mile away. But in LA, they were like ninjas with cameras. They blended into the background until a celebrity tripped the wire, then they swarmed en masse out of nowhere.

"You look older," was the first thing Sammy said as we walked into the restaurant.

"You don't," I replied, being totally truthful. Sammy really did look amazing. Smelled terrific too. When she hugged me hello in the hotel lobby, the familiar scent of her skin gave me a sense-memory buzz. When the hug was over, Sam grabbed me by my shoulders, looked me in the eyes, and gave me an affectionate shake. "Max, you have no idea how much I've missed you," she said, then she came in for a second squeeze. If I'd had any doubts as to whether I would still feel that old pull of attraction, they were gone. It was going to be a rough night.

"How's Johnny?" I asked Sammy as we settled in at our table. "Is he going to do the DVD commentary?"

"I told the studio that there's nothing wrong with his voice," she said. "But between you and me, I don't know. He gets tired so easily. He's fifty-five, but he's got the stamina of a ninety-year-old. He falls asleep in the middle of conversations. Seriously, you'll be talking to him and suddenly you hear snoring." Sammy took a long sip of wine. "The thing is, Johnny *really* wants to do it. I keep telling him that his legacy is going to be huge whether he does a DVD commentary or not. He's Johnny Mars, for Christ's sake. But he's got his heart set on it."

"He's lucky he's got you looking out for him," I said. "I'm sure you convinced the studio."

"Well, it wasn't all selfless, coming to LA," Samantha said, taking another sip. "To be honest, I really needed to escape. I hardly ever get to leave the apartment anymore. Especially now, since that photographer got that shot of Johnny in the garage. It's like all the other paparazzi smell blood in the water. They're in a frenzy trying to get another picture. I can't step out on our balcony without flashbulbs going off. Remember that photographer in the black SUV? He's *still* following me around. It's such a relief to get away. I feel like I can finally breathe."

"You know, we have paparazzi in LA, too," I told her. "They're right outside the hotel."

"Yeah, but in LA I don't feel so exposed," Sammy said, a blissful smile on her face. "I don't feel as conspicuous. Look around, nobody is staring at me. It's like I'm not even here. I feel free!"

"Oh, they notice, all right," I said. "It's just that people in LA have more practice pretending not to stare at celebrities in restaurants. I guarantee you, right now the name 'Samantha Mars' is being whispered at every table in the place."

"Oh, shut up," Sammy said. "Don't spoil this for me. You're in enough trouble already for leaving New York. I hate the fact that you're thousands of miles away. I know we didn't get to see each other that often, but it was comforting knowing you were close. In case I needed you. You know me better than anyone in the world, Max. Better even than Johnny." She reached across the table and squeezed my hand, and didn't let go for the longest time. It was the most intense skin-on-skin contact I'd had with

Samantha in years. "You know, if I hadn't met him doing that Chekhov play in Concord, you and I would be an old married couple by now."

A waiter arrived with menus, giving me a moment to collect my thoughts. You know how in cartoons a little angel and devil appear on opposite shoulders and argue over what someone should do? My shoulder angel must have been caught in traffic on the Santa Monica Freeway, because the only one whispering in my ear was the red guy with horns and a tail. "She's lonely," he said. "She's vulnerable. This is it, Max. This is your chance. She held your hand! She's practically begging for it!" Then my mini angel finally showed up. He was sweaty and panting. "Sorry I'm late," he said, bending over to catch his breath. "Sammy *is* lonely, she *is* vulnerable," he said. "And if you took advantage of her, how could you ever look at yourself in the mirror again? She's your oldest and dearest friend, Max. Do you really want to screw that up? Besides, aren't we getting ahead of ourselves? Just because Samantha held your hand doesn't mean she's inviting you to commit adultery with her."

Samantha ordered the coconut mustard seed sustainable Chilean sea bass. I had the mango-infused mallard drizzled with chutney reduction. Before the waiter left, Sam asked him to bring another bottle of wine.

"I love Johnny, I really do," Samantha went on. "But it's so hard sometimes. Every day is such a struggle. And every day is the same. There's no relief. And no hope that it's going to get better. People keep telling me how strong I am. I'm supposed to be Saint Samantha. It makes me want to scream. I'm not as strong as people think. I'm no saint. You of all people know that, Max." She refilled her wineglass. If I didn't know better, I would have thought she was trying to get drunk. "What about you?" she said, abruptly changing the subject. "What's going on with you? Tell me about your love life. Are you seeing anyone?"

"At the moment, I'm between engagements," I said, watching the devil and angel wrestling across the table-cloth. I thought about telling Sam about Eliska, but what was there to say? That I was chasing after another girl I had no chance of getting? "I guess I just haven't found the right woman yet."

"Why *is* that?" Sammy pressed. "I mean, you date all these girls—how come you never fall in love with any of them?"

"I fell in love once, remember? You were there."

"And you haven't fallen for anyone since?" Sammy asked.

"No, but I'm not dead yet," I said.

"I'm the only girl you've ever been in love with," Sammy repeated, almost to herself, as if that incredibly obvious fact had never fully dawned on her before. She gave me a big, warm smile. "That makes me want to cry," she said. "That breaks my heart in the best possible way."

"Well, don't get a big head over it," I said, pouring myself a large glass of wine. It had taken thirteen years, scores of late-night phone calls, and Lord knows how many bottles of merlot over dinners just like this one for Sammy to figure out how I felt about her. Now that she was finally seeing what had always been right in front of her eyes, she was looking at me in a way she hadn't since we were in our twenties. My palms began to sweat. "It's the clown nose you wore when you were doing children's theater," I feebly joked. "I've never been able to get over it."

Sammy reached across the table and took my hand again. "This is LA," she said. "I'm sure we can find a clown nose somewhere."

The devil was stabbing the angel with a salad fork.

I'm not going to go into all the gory, romance novel details. How Sammy invited me up to her hotel suite. How the second the door closed I took her into my arms and kissed her. How my heart pounded as she led me to the bedroom and my fingers trembled as I fumbled with the buttons on her blouse. I could tap out thousands of purple words describing every pulsing, throbbing minute.

But it wasn't like that. It felt more like a homecoming. Or a return from Babylonian exile. After years of wandering in the desert, I'd finally found my way back to the promised land. I'd fantasized about it for so long, it was surreal to actually experience it. I couldn't believe it was really happening. Being with Sammy again was both exquisitely familiar and breathtakingly new. The softness of her touch, the sweetness of her taste, the rhythms of her breathing—it was like biting into a Proustian cookie from an erotic bakery. When Sammy gently nibbled my earlobe, I could have wept with joy. That little maneuver drove me crazy back when we were teenagers. I couldn't believe she remembered.

In a lot of ways, it reminded me of our first times together, when we snuck around behind our parents' backs for secret sleepover dates. All these years later, we were still slinking off to share forbidden fruit. The difference, though, was that we weren't so innocent anymore. We'd grown up. We'd seen this movie before. When I looked into Sammy's eyes, I used to see hope and joy and yearning for the adventure of the future. Now I saw fatigue and sorrow and longing for the past.

When I woke up the following morning, I was alone and hungover in Sammy's bed at the Shui. I sat up and looked around. Our clothes were strewn all over the floor. A lamp on the bedside table had been knocked over. There was pretentious stenciling on the wall above my head. DREAM, it said. No, I thought. This time I'm wide awake. Then I heard Sammy's voice coming from the living room. She was talking on the phone. "Yes, it's going to be fine, I promise," I heard her saying. "The studio is really excited about you doing the commentary. They're going to have technicians come to the apartment with all the equipment. You won't have to go anywhere . . ."

Johnny. I'd forgotten about him. Little bubbles of guilt began floating to the surface of my consciousness. I tried to push them down. I thought about what Sammy said in the elevator on the way up to her room. Her theory, she explained as she nuzzled my neck, was that sleeping with me would be a less egregious form of adultery, since we'd already slept together so many times before she got married. "What's one or two more?" she said. "I mean, who's counting?" It was sloppy math, based on drunken logic, but in the moment, with Sammy's breath on my chest, it all added up.

In the sobering light of morning, though, as I lay in

Sammy's bed eavesdropping on her phone call with her husband, I reassessed the situation. You didn't need teams of Swiss psychologists working round the clock to figure out what was going on in Sammy's head. She *was* lonely. She *was* vulnerable. She needed to escape, if only for a night. She loved the man she married but, despite what she told Larry King, he wasn't functioning in that department anymore. Sammy was only human. Even saints have needs.

I, of course, had been plotting and scheming and praying for this night for more than a decade. But it's one thing to game out theoretical counterfactuals in the privacy of your own skull; it's quite another to wake up in the real world and find yourself in a married woman's bed. What was going to happen next? Would Sammy march into the bedroom and announce that it had all been a terrible mistake, let's forget the whole thing ever happened, order room service before you go? Or was this the start of something more? Did I even want something more? Now that it was an actual, genuine possibility, did I truly want her back? After so much time and distance and one-sided longing between us, I couldn't tell anymore. Besides, what if we got caught? With paparazzi hiding behind every bush, that was a real danger. I could see my picture in the papers, the jerk who broke up Johnny and Sammy. I'd become a tabloid punching bag, the Yoko Ono of celebrity brain cancer.

And then there was Eliska. Had I betrayed her by sleeping with Sammy? I couldn't decide. It sure *felt* like I had been unfaithful. I thought about all the others I'd hurt over the years, the vast conga line of women I had unceremoniously dumped when things started getting too serious. They were the casualties of my obsession with Samantha. I didn't want Eliska to be another. Yet here I was, in another woman's bed. In Sammy's bed. I ducked under the covers and groaned.

"Sorry about that," Samantha said when she stepped back into the bedroom wrapped only in a fluffy terrycloth robe. She sat down on the side of the bed. "Are you okay?" she asked, grinning awkwardly. "Are you feeling weird about, you know, last night?"

"Um, no, not at all," I said, not terribly convincingly. It's funny, but in my fantasies, all my relationship issues vanished into thin air the minute Sammy and I got back together. After all, she was the one who gave me those issues in the first place. But it wasn't working out that way.

"I know I should be feeling horrible," Sammy said. "I know I should be wracked with guilt. I'm sure I will be at some point. A big freak-out is coming, I'm sure. But right now, I feel great." She lay down on the bed next to me and rested her head on my chest. "I feel like I'm seventeen again. I feel like we've gone back in time. Like we've got our whole lives ahead of us again."

Something was terribly wrong. I didn't feel that way at all. I still felt love for her, of course. But something was different, something was definitely not right. I didn't know what, but I knew I needed to get out of that hotel room to figure it out.

17

There was an e-mail from Eliska waiting for me when I got home from my night with Sammy. "I have a confession," she wrote. "You are not my first pen pal. When I was ten, our teacher gave us the addresses of children all over the Soviet Union. We were supposed to write them in order to improve our Russian language skills. My pen pal was named Illya and he lived in Leningrad. Most kids wrote only one or two letters before they got bored, but Illya and I kept writing and writing. We ended up writing each other for almost a year. But then, when Illya turned twelve, he got a girlfriend, and he stopped writing me. I guess you could say he was my first heartbreak."

There was a smiley emoticon indicating that last line was a joke. Or maybe it was Abraham Lincoln kissing a penguin—I could never really tell what Eliska's emoticons were supposed to be. I read her words several more times, imagining Eliska as a young girl at the height of the Cold War, trapped behind the Iron Curtain in Czechoslovakia, peering out the window of a snow-encrusted dacha, waiting anxiously for a letter from a boy in Leningrad. I could practically hear *Doctor Zhivago*'s theme music. Under normal circumstances, I'd have written her back right away, but I clicked the e-mail closed. These weren't normal circumstances. I would have to find time for Eliska later.

I was freaking out over Sammy. Worse, I was freaking out over the fact that I was freaking out. I couldn't figure out what the hell my problem was. Hadn't I wanted this for years? Then why couldn't I shake the nagging feeling that I had made a big mistake? Of course, I always had a nagging feeling I'd made a big mistake whenever I got close to a woman, but this felt different. This wasn't the same old gamophobia. I wasn't imagining thick ankles or hallucinating veiny arms; this wasn't about my fear of intimacy or inability to commit. This time I was pretty sure I really had screwed up.

I kept thinking about what Sam had said—how I knew her better than anybody. I realized that was only half true. I knew everything there was to know about twenty-four-year-old Sammy, from how many pumps of butter she liked on her movie popcorn to what sort of bristles she preferred on her toothbrush. Presumably, at thirty-seven, she still enjoyed three pumps and a medium-hard brush, but in other ways she was a completely different person. So was I. We weren't candy-eyed tweens sharing ice cream in a sofa sleeper in a Greenwich Village studio anymore. We were supposed to be grown-ups.

I realized something else, as well. All those years I spent lying in wait, posing as Sammy's platonic buddy as part of my elaborate ruse to win her back—turned out I wasn't entirely pretending. When she called at two a.m. to talk about Johnny's latest medical crisis, or some career setback of her own, or whatever, I wasn't feigning my sympathy. I genuinely did care. I truly wanted to be there for her to lean on. All along I may have been scheming and plotting, but that didn't mean I was faking my feelings. I barely noticed it was happening, but over countless late-night calls and catching-up dinners, Sammy and I got close in a way I hadn't anticipated. Maybe she wasn't really the One—maybe she never had been—but she was something else that was almost as rare and nearly as valuable. A real friend.

I just hoped I hadn't messed it up with a one-night stand at the Shui.

I didn't bother to check for an e-mail from Sammy—she was still on her flight back to New York. But I knew there wouldn't be an e-mail even after she landed. Sammy hated e-mail. When it came to letter writing, she believed in the sanctity of stationery. When she contacted me again it would either be with a handwritten note or, more likely, a late-night phone call. I had no idea what was going through her mind. She didn't offer any clues when I left her packing her bags in her hotel suite. She simply gave me a long, slow hug at the door, kissed me gently on the lips, then stepped back and adjusted the belt on her bathrobe. "Don't forget to write," she said, smiling. She hadn't used that line on me in years, but it was her favorite parting back in our college days, when she was still encouraging me to become a journalist.

But I knew what had to be done. As her friend, I couldn't complicate her life with an affair that she only thought she wanted because she was lonely. I had to nip it in the bud before it went any further. I took a deep breath and made myself a promise: no matter what Sammy was thinking, no matter what she might be planning for us, I had to be the strong one and do the right thing.

Meanwhile, there was an e-mail from Carla. She was assigning me an interview with Suki Monroe, who-ever that was. This was starting to happen a lot; Carla would assign me a story on a celebrity I had never heard of before. It seemed that nobody wanted to read about old-fashioned movie stars anymore. Instead, in 2008, a brand-new crop of "reality" stars with funny, unfamiliar names—like Kardashian and Gosselin and Obama—were sucking up all the oxygen in the media. Every season, I felt myself falling more and more out of step with my once beloved pop culture. Worse than out of step—half the time I was horrified by what I was seeing. Movies based on theme park rides. TV dating shows for midgets. Taylor Hicks. I was just shy of thirty-eight, but already I was aging out of the target demographic. The culture was moving on without me.

Suki Monroe, it turned out, was indeed a reality star, of a sort. She was the flamboyant, hugely success-ful restaurateur who had just opened a new theme eatery on Hollywood Boulevard called Celebrity. It was one of those brilliant ideas that makes you wonder why nobody had thought of it before: a place where unfamous paying customers could experience, for a couple of hours, what it was like to be Jack Nicholson. From the moment you arrived at Celebrity's red-carpeted entrance (where fake paparazzi pretended to take your picture) you were treated like a member of the A-list. You'd get ushered past a line of waiting customers (or, rather, a bunch of extras being paid to look like customers) and escorted directly to your table, the best in the house (like every table at Celebrity). At least once during your meal, you'd be approached by a (paid) fan asking for an autograph. "In the future," promised Celebrity's Warholian advertising slogan, "everybody will be famous for three courses."

"I know you don't normally write about restaurants," Carla wrote in her e-mail assigning me the story, "but this seems right up your alley. It's all about your favorite subject—fame! The interview is set for Friday night. Dinner at Celebrity. *Bon appétit.*"

She was not Asian, nor was she related in any way to Marilyn. Her real name was Janice Smith, but she changed it to the more attention-grabbing Suki Monroe when, at seventeen, she left Ohio for Los Angeles to pursue a career as an actress. When that didn't work out, Suki pursued producers. She ended up marrying and divorcing three of them over a period of fifteen years. With the money she made from those profitable failures she opened her first restaurant in West Hollywood in 1996. It was called Formaggio alla Griglia, and it wowed the LA food world by giving the lowly grilled cheese sandwich a gourmet makeover and turning it into a sexy, decadent treat. Three years later, Suki jumped into LA's cutthroat high-end cupcake business by opening her first Shut Your Pie Hole cupcake shop. Within two years, she controlled Los Angeles's small baked goods trade with the iron grip of a mafia boss.

From everything that I read about her in the clip file, she was as flaky as she was formidable. For starters, she wore a turban, not a look you saw a lot of in LA since Tallulah Bankhead passed away. For another, she was such a devoted animal activist she once tried to ban fur-wearing customers from eating in her restaurants (she reluctantly rescinded the edict after the *Los Angeles Times* pointed out how many swine were slaughtered every month to fill croque monsieur sandwiches at Formaggio alla Griglia). But Suki could also be ruthless. A few years back, she made a play for the ultimate culinary trophy in Hollywood—catering the Governors Ball at the Oscars. When Wolfgang Puck beat back her challenge, Suki took it hard. In an interview with *Los Angeles Magazine,* she dismissively referred to Puck as "Ronald McDonald with a Düsseldorf accent." As far as I could tell from the clips, she still hadn't apologized.

When I arrived at Celebrity on Friday night at 7:30, I couldn't help but be impressed. The fake paparazzi at the entrance went berserk when I stepped onto the red carpet, snapping pretend pictures and begging me to pose for their prop cameras. Of course, they also went berserk over the elderly tourist couple who arrived before me, and over everybody else with reservations that night. The extras pretending to be customers in line for a table were pretty convincing, too, although they had the easiest acting jobs in Hollywood. All they had to do was stand behind velvet ropes and gawk with wide-eyed astonishment as "celebrities" filed into the dining room. When I got to the hostess station, there was a moment of confusion when the hostess realized I was meeting Suki herself for dinner. That made me an actual VIP. She was trying to figure out how to suck up to me for real, instead of just make-believe.

Suki kept me waiting at our table for fifteen minutes, which was about average when interviewing famous people, even famous restaurateurs. I was glad for the time it gave me to watch Celebrity in motion, to observe the clockwork of the operation. I noticed, for instance, a blond woman in a blue dress get up from her corner table and walk over to another table halfway across the room. She asked the delighted diners for their autographs, and jumped and yelped with over-the-top enthusiasm when they signed her pad. Less than five minutes later, she did exactly the same thing to another table. Like the fake paparazzi outside, the fake autograph hound in the blue dress might as well have been an animatronic robot. She repeated the same thirty-second script over and over again. I was truly in awe of what Suki had accomplished here: she had turned fame into a post-ironic theme ride.

"I'm Suki Monroe," she said, sneaking up on me from behind. "Sorry to keep you waiting."

I had to admit, the black silk turban took years off her face. Or maybe it was Botox. Around her throat, a two-carat red diamond glittered in a platinum choker like a tracheotomy by Tiffany. She was an attractive, extremely well-put-together forty-six-year-old multimillionaire. From the clips I'd read, I knew she could also be a prickly interview subject. But even for a famous diva of the LA foodie scene, coverage in a major national magazine like KNOW was a big deal (after all, Time had been running puff pieces on

Wolfgang for years). So Suki was on her best behavior. Better than best: the truth is, we had one of the mostly bluntly honest conversations about fame I'd ever had with anyone who ever had any. Carla was spot-on—Suki was right up my alley.

"Do you know why everybody wants to be famous?" Suki asked me while we nibbled on salmon canapé appetizers. "Have you ever thought about fame, I mean *really* thought about it? What fame is exactly? Why people are so obsessed with it?"

"As a matter of fact—" I started to say.

"I'll tell you why," she went on. "Fame is the ultimate status symbol. And status, when you cut through all the crap, is what life is all about. Everybody wants to feel special. Everybody wants to think that they're better than the next guy. Everybody wants to be higher up on the food chain than their neighbors. And there's nobody higher on the food chain in our world than celebrities."

"It's interesting that you say that because—"

"Most people in their daily lives never get to feel special in that way," Suki rolled on. "Most people never even encounter a celebrity in their lives. And if they are lucky enough to see one, or even shake one's hand, it's a big moment. They take pictures to show their friends. It's like some of that celebrity specialness has rubbed off on them. It gives them bragging rights. It gives them status: 'I've met Jimmy Kimmel, have you?'"

I felt the phone in my pocket vibrating. I wondered if it might be Samantha. It had been four days since our night together at the Shui, and I hadn't heard from her yet, by letter or by phone. But it was only 8:20 in LA, 11:20 in

New York. That was a little early for Sammy to be calling. Unless sleeping together had bumped me up to an earlier calling time. I did my best to ignore the vibrating while I listened to Suki explain fame.

"What we're doing here at Celebrity," she said, "is democratizing fame. We're giving everyone a chance to experience it. For once in their ordinary lives, normal folk get to feel like the most important people in the room. They get to have the status. And even though everyone knows it's fake, that they aren't really celebrities, they still get a rush out of it. They still get to feel what it's like. They get to be famous without having to do anything to earn it. Except, of course," she added with a grin, "pay the check at the end of the night."

"Yes, but isn't there something sort of sad about that?" I said, finally managing to squeeze in a question. "Doesn't it say something kind of pathetic about human beings— that fame is the thing that gives us the most status? Rather than, say, intelligence or empathy or bravery?" I could feel my phone vibrating again. Jesus, Sammy, hold your horses.

"You're probably right," Suki answered. "But it's human nature. People want to be famous because it gives them the illusion that their life is important. That it actually matters that they're alive. That even after they die, some part of them will live after them. Fame is really a state of grace, only with money and power and beautiful lovers." A waiter slipped next to Suki to deliver her a note on a silver tray. She unfolded the paper, skimmed its contents, and looked up at me with a smile. "I'm so sorry— I know this is rude—but there's a phone call I really must take," she said, getting up from the table. "It's Jon Bon Jovi. A real celebrity! We're doing an event for him. Just give me a moment."

While Suki was gone, I pulled out my phone to see if Sammy had left a message. But it wasn't Sammy who'd been calling. It was Robin's 323 number in Silver Lake. She was still writing for *DINKs,* but had finally moved out of my loft and rented a small house in the hipster enclave east of Hollywood. She even had a new girlfriend. I assumed that was what the calls must be about—Robin had had her heart broken for the umpteenth time. I decided to deal with it later and was about to slip the phone back into my pocket when it started vibrating again. It was Robin calling for the third time. I answered.

"Are you all right?" Robin asked, sounding more anxious than I'd ever heard her before. "Where are you? Do you need me?"

"I'm fine," I said, puzzled. "I'm at that new restaurant Celebrity. Do you know about it? It's really wild. You get to be a movie star for a night—"

"Max," Robin interrupted me, "you haven't heard, have you?"

"Heard what? What are you talking about?"

"Oh fuck," Robin moaned into the phone. "I can't believe I'm the one who has to tell you this. This so sucks." Her voice had that reedy warble it always got just before she burst into tears. "Max, something really horrible has happened. There's been a car accident in New York. On the West Side Highway. A really bad one. It's all over the news. Samantha was in the car. She's dead, Max. Samantha is dead."

I don't recall hanging up the phone. But I do remember that at first I didn't feel a thing. "How odd," I said to myself. "Why am I not reacting?" And then, suddenly, the Earth tilted thirty degrees on its axis. The restaurant began spinning around me as if I were in the center of a carousel. I could hear people talking and laughing, but I couldn't focus on where their voices were coming from. I reached for a linen napkin and, as discreetly as I could, retched in it. When I looked up, there was a blond woman in a blue dress standing in front of me, holding out a pad and pen.

"Excuse me," she said, acting very nervous. "I'm so sorry to bother you. But I'm such a huge fan of your work. You've been such an inspiration to me and to so many others. Would it be okay if I asked for your autograph?"

I must have had a complete dissociative breakdown. I could barely remember who I was, let alone understand why this strange woman wanted my autograph. I took her pad and pen and scribbled the only name I could think of. With flawless penmanship, I wrote, "Samantha Mars."

18

After somehow managing to get home, I spent the next three days holed up watching wall-to-wall coverage of Samantha's death on the cable news channels. Details of the crash were coming in drip by drip, like Chinese water torture.

Sammy had been on her way to Westchester to have dinner with her parents. For reasons nobody yet understood, instead of taking a chauffeured town car, her usual mode of transport, Sammy decided to drive herself in the Mars's seldom-used BMW sports wagon. The minute she left the garage, she was trailed by a black Ford SUV—license plate 944BBDC—driven by a self-described "photojournalist" named Andrew Leighton. According to CNN, Leighton had a long history as an aggressive paparazzo going as far back as 1993, when John Kennedy Jr. and Daryl Hannah filed a restraining order against him. According to MSNBC, Sammy had complained to friends about Leighton's black SUV, saying she felt like she was being stalked.

At some point while driving north on the West Side Highway, Samantha must have finally got fed up with being followed. She attempted to elude Leighton. A witness told Fox News that Sammy's car abruptly accelerated, weaving between traffic in the double lanes, but that Leighton continued pursuing at high speed. Just after Sammy passed the Riverside Drive exit, before reaching the Henry Hudson Bridge, she lost control of her vehicle. It swerved into an embankment and spun around. Leighton slammed on his breaks, but not in time. He plowed head-on into Samantha's driver-side door, crushing the BMW like a soda can, killing Sammy instantly. Leighton's SUV flipped on impact and collided with a pillar. He may have taken a few minutes to die.

I kept waiting to wake up. I could actually feel my mind pushing back against the fact that Sammy was dead, blocking the thought by any means necessary. Any minute now, I told myself, Sammy was going to appear on TV to announce that it had all been an Andy Kaufman–style hoax. She had jumped out of the BMW just in time. Some part of me must have known that she really was dead— I could see an avalanche of grief heading my way—but I clung to denial for as long as I possibly could. Which wasn't very long.

Watching it all unfold on TV was beyond surreal. Sammy's death completely took over the news channels. A paparazzo had been involved in a celebrity spouse's death. That was enough to make it a major story. Except this was no ordinary celebrity spouse. This was Saint Samantha, the poster girl of matrimonial loyalty and sacrifice. The media went nuts. Comparisons to Lady Di's crash in Paris ten years earlier were all over the airwaves. One cable anchor went so far as to awkwardly proclaim Sammy "America's people's princess." There was footage of fans laying flowers near the site on the West Side Highway where the collision occurred. There were long shots of Johnny's apartment building, where the star was said to be mourning his loss. There were interviews with angry politicians promising crackdowns on "the paparazzi menace." And, of course, there was endless video of Sammy, going to movie openings with Johnny, attending black-tie medical research fund-raisers, that ubiquitous home movie clip of ten-year-old Sammy playing on a beach in Cape Cod.

Robin hovered, phoning multiple times. "I bet you couldn't have guessed in a million years that this would be the way the story ended," she said, having a philosophical moment while I watched a computer-generated animated re-creation of the accident on CNN for the hundredth time. I hadn't had a chance to tell Robin what happened with Sammy the week before at the Shui. Even though I'd been having a meltdown over it, a tiny part of me had been looking forward to bragging. After all, I'd been talking to Robin about getting Sammy back throughout our whole friendship. Now, though, I wanted to keep my night with Sam to myself. It seemed too precious a memory to share.

My dad phoned. You'd think that after his experience losing my mother in a car crash, he would have had something soothing and wise to say. But it was precisely because of his experience that he knew there were no words for a time like this. "Son, I'm so sorry for your loss" was the best he could come up with. Then he put his new lady friend, Madge, on the phone to offer her condolences. "So, how did you know her?" she asked. Still, I appreciated the call.

Carla telephoned, too, although it turned out she had an ulterior motive. "Max, how horrible for you," she said. "I know you were friends with Samantha. You were close, weren't you? You know what might help? Maybe if you wrote something for the magazine about her. It might be cathartic, don't you think?"

"Carla," I said, "I don't think I'm going to do much writing for a while. Especially about celebrities."

"You want to take a break from writing?" she asked. "I'm not sure that's such a great idea, Max. How long a break were you thinking?"

"Forever," I said. "Forever sounds about right."

After three days, I decided it was time to switch off the TV. It took Herculean strength, but I pushed myself into the shower and scrounged up some fresh clothing. I hadn't eaten much since throwing up at Celebrity. Robin had brought over a pizza the night before, but it sat untouched on the butcher-block counter in my kitchen. I took out a cold piece and sniffed, then put it back in its box. I looked in the refrigerator, but there was nothing I wanted. Then I opened my laptop and checked my e-mail. There was an ad for discount Viagra, a sale announcement at Fred Segal, a couple of work-related items, and a message from Eliska wondering where I'd been and why I hadn't answered her last e-mail. It would have been so easy to write her a short note explaining that a close friend had passed away and that I'd get back in touch with her when I could. But I just didn't have the energy.

Then I saw an e-mail from Sammy. My heart jumped. But, of course, it wasn't from Sammy. It was from one of her sisters. She was using Sam's computer, she explained, to let people in Samantha's contacts list know that there was going to be a memorial service in New York in one week. Did I want to be put on the guest list? I'd never heard of a funeral with a "guest list" before, but I responded that, yes, by all means, I'd be there. I wondered how many other of Sammy's contacts were getting posthumous e-mails. I was a little surprised Sam even had a contact list, given that she did so little e-mailing. And then, like a light flipping on in my brain, it occurred to me: I hadn't been to the mailbox in three days.

Sure enough, mixed in with the cable bill and the supermarket flyers, there was a small envelope with Sammy's round, feminine writing on it. I turned it over in my hands and examined it for a long moment before tearing it open. I was keenly aware that inside were Samantha's last words to me. It was postmarked the day before her death.

"Dear Max," she wrote in a short note. "Dinner was lovely. After dinner was even lovelier. Amazingly, I'm still not freaking out—not yet, anyway. I hope you aren't, either. There are so many things I want to say to you, but I can't think straight right now. Life is so much more complicated than when we were kids. But whatever ends up happening, Max, please know that I love you. I always have and always will."

Sammy's memorial service was held at the Magistrate Theater, the very spot where, ten years earlier, I attended the premiere of *Canterbury's Pilgrim* and came as close as I ever had to meeting Johnny Mars in the flesh. There weren't any roving klieg lights or red carpets or even very many popping flashbulbs—the paparazzi wisely kept their distance—but in every other way it looked just like a movie opening. Celebrities were everywhere.

I knew that I would finally meet Johnny Mars at Sammy's memorial, and I spent most of the flight to New York wondering what I would say to him. There had been so many different things I'd wanted to tell him over so many years. As a kid, thrilling to his exploits on the screen, I wanted to cheer him on with all my teenage heart. In my twenties, after he stole Sammy, I wanted to rage at him with all my broken heart. In my thirties, after Johnny got sick, I wanted to tell him how sorry I was, how much I pitied him. But now, with Sammy gone, I had no idea what I wanted to say. I wasn't sure how I felt about him. I wasn't sure how I felt about anything.

I'd been to a lot of celeb-packed events in my time, but never a funeral. Under the shadow of death, the rituals of fame and exclusivity seemed even emptier and more ridiculous than ever. After being ushered in by clipboard-toting gatekeepers, mourners picked up their tickets at the box office window, along with a program printed on luxurious linen paper. On the cover was a picture of Samantha. Inside was a list of the people who would be stepping to the podium to share their memories of her. Christina Ricci, John Travolta, Sandra Bullock, Bruce Willis, Sylvester Stallone, Tommy Lee Jones—there were more stars appearing onstage at Sammy's memorial than at the Oscars. It made me want to gag.

People were milling around, filling the hall with the murmur of hundreds of whispered conversations. So I milled too. I spotted DeeDee Devry chatting with Rupert Everett and Leonard Cox talking with Ben Affleck. Even Chuck Fuse, Johnny's replacement, was there, with his arm around Jay Moses. I didn't see Johnny anywhere, but I knew he had to be close. Eventually I spotted Sammy's family, her mom and dad and her two sisters, huddled together on the other side of the orchestra section. They were the only ones not working the room, just sitting quietly, waiting for the ceremony to begin. I was about to go over to give them all hugs when the lights in the theater dimmed and people began taking their seats.

"You again!" the man in the seat next to mine said when I settled in. It took me a second to find the face underneath the overgrown beard and mustache, but it was the actor Alistair Lyon. I remembered reading that he'd been cast as the lead in *Ulysses S.*, a biopic about General Grant, which perhaps explained the forest of facial hair. "We must be karmically connected," he said. "We keep bumping into each other in the oddest places. How did you know Samantha Mars? Did you interview her?"

"No," I answered. "I never interviewed her. She was my girlfriend. Until Johnny came along."

"I don't understand," Alistair said. "Your girlfriend was Samantha Mars?"

"She wasn't Samantha *Mars* at the time, but yes. One minute I was living with her, the next she was married to Johnny Mars."

"That's extraordinary," Lyon said. "An action star stole your love. That must have been rough to get over."

I left that unanswered—I wasn't about to open up to a movie star on this of all occasions. "What about you— how did you know Samantha?"

"Oh, I never met her," Lyon answered.

"So you're friends with Johnny?"

"Not exactly friends," he said. "We've met a few times. I'm just here to pay my respects. What these poor people have been through. It's so tragic it's almost biblical. She was literally killed by fame."

The ceremony opened with Sheryl Crow singing "Amazing Grace." I tried to figure out how Crow knew Sammy, then remembered that she'd sung the title song for *Yankee Doodle Deadly,* one of the Montana films Johnny made in the late nineties. Then Willis came out and told a story about meeting Sammy on the set of Johnny's last completed Montana movie, *Independence Slay,* in which Willis did a cameo as a Ukrainian uranium dealer. I began to realize that, except for Ricci, who had worked with Sammy on *Losers Weepers,* all the stars on the stage had met Sam through Johnny. They were his pals—and, in Alistair's case, mere acquaintances—not hers. It made me wonder if Sammy had had any friends of her own since becoming Mrs. Mars. It didn't seem so. For the first time, it began to dawn on me just how lonely and isolated Sammy may have been, even before Johnny's illness. Her late-night calls—maybe those weren't mini vacations. Maybe they were more like lifelines. How had I not seen that? I'd been so busy obsessing about my own problems, I never gave a thought to hers.

If I hadn't been consumed by my secret plot to win Sammy back, if I had just accepted that we were never going to be anything more (or less) than lifelong friends, I might have been more sensitive. But all along, I'd been making the same mistake I always made with Samantha. Sure, I figured out how to bring flowers and pick better gifts—I never again gave her a *Man from U.N.C.L.E.* boxed set, that's for sure—but I still hadn't learned to see beyond my own personal desires. All I wanted was to make Sammy love me again, whether that was what Sammy wanted or not. I never thought about her feelings. I was selfish and self-centered. And now it was too late to do anything about it.

I peered over the hairdos in the theater, scanning for Johnny. He was usually easy to spot in a crowd, even in a wheelchair. But he didn't seem to be there. From what I'd heard during dinner at the Shui, as well as what I'd been reading in the gossip columns, Mars's health had been slipping even before Sammy had been killed. There were rumors that he'd been suffering from bouts of memory loss, forgetting even his own name. I guess I could understand why he might not show at his wife's memorial service. Part of me was relieved; I could stop worrying about what to say to him. But another part was disappointed. I'd been shadowboxing with Johnny for a decade. He had been such a major force in my life, but he was still as two-dimensional to me as his character on the screen. I was finally going to get to experience the actual man.

I looked over at Alistair. He was dabbing his eyes with a pocket square. In fact, all around the theater, famous people were sniffling and weeping. Even if they hadn't known Sammy as well as I had, even if they hadn't known her at all, Sammy's death had clearly touched them. The strange thing was, I wasn't crying. I was sad to the bone, to be sure. I was totally shattered. Next to her family, I knew Sam better than anyone in the theater. But no tears. Not yet.

About thirty minutes into the ceremony, while Aimee Mann was onstage singing "The Last Mile of the Way," I felt a tap on my shoulder. I turned and saw a young woman in a starched white nurse's outfit. She knelt in the aisle next to me and whispered, "Are you Max Lerner?" I nodded yes. "Would you please come with me?" I looked over at Alistair Lyon, who'd been watching with curiosity. He just shrugged his shoulders. He had no idea what was going on, either. I stood and followed the nurse up the aisle toward the back of the theater, watching her walk in her big, ugly white shoes. She guided me into the lobby and through a door marked NO ENTRY, then down a long hallway toward the backstage dressing rooms. We passed a women's restroom; the "W" had fallen off so that the sign on the door read OMEN. We finally came to another door, with a star painted on it. The nurse gave it a quick couple of raps, turned the knob, and led me inside.

It was a small, run-down space with a makeup table and a lighted mirror against one wall and a beat-up old leatherette loveseat against another. In the middle of the

room, slumped in an electric wheelchair, was a shriveled, ancient-looking mummy of a man. It took me a
beat or two to realize who it was. "Is there anything you
need?" the nurse gently asked her patient. He waved her
away with the one functional part of his body—his still-
muscular left arm—and the nurse went back out the door,
leaving us alone together. For the first time in my life, I
was face-to-face with Johnny Mars.

Nothing I'd seen on TV or read in the papers had prepared me for just how desiccated Johnny looked in person. He had lost at least half his once-hulking body mass;
at most, he weighed one hundred pounds. His legs were
as thin as broomsticks. His face was so gaunt and gray
and lifeless, it was startling to see it move. The only part
of him that still looked vaguely alive, aside from his one
good arm, were his eyes, which Mars now trained on me
with terrifying intensity. I nervously adjusted my necktie
while I waited for him to speak. "You are Max Lerner?"
His lips barely moved but his voice still rumbled like a subway under a sidewalk. I nodded my head yes. Mars continued staring at my face for what seemed like an eternity.
Finally, he spoke again.

"Samantha cared a lot about you," he said. "She was
always talking about you. She said you were a great friend
to her."

I had to bite down hard to keep from breaking into
sobs. I cleared my throat. "You know," I told him, "there
was a time when I hated your guts."

"I stole your girlfriend," he said. "I don't blame you."

"No," I said, finally grasping something I should have
figured out a decade ago. Standing in front of Mars, the

man who'd gone from boyhood idol to nemesis to object of my confused pity, it all suddenly became clear. All the resentment and anger fell away, and I suddenly saw that I hadn't been good enough for Sammy. Not because I wasn't an action star, not because I couldn't offer her penthouse apartments and ranches in Wyoming, not because of anything like that—but because I didn't know what real love was. Maybe I couldn't know when I was in my early twenties. But I knew it now. Watching Sammy as Mrs. Mars had taught it to me.

"You didn't steal her," I said. "I lost her. You were just lucky enough to find her."

Mars's facial muscles began twitching, his mouth contorting spastically. It took me a second or two to figure out what was happening. He was trying to smile.

19

I went through the motions. I got up every morning and started the day with a bike ride on the path along Venice Beach. I stopped by the bodega on Carroll Canal for an orange juice and *Variety*. I drove to the bureau in Brentwood to check my mailbox for press releases and swag. I interviewed Tom Cruise. Again. It was exactly the same life I'd been living before Sammy died. But it felt somehow different. It felt stupid.

I no longer found fame fascinating. On the contrary, my decade-long pseudoscientific research into the mysteries of celebrity now seemed an idiotic waste of time. What did it matter if fame was a disease or a drug or a status symbol? Who cared? It was no great riddle why people turned their heads when Jack Nicholson entered the dining room of a restaurant. It's because he's Jack fucking Nicholson. Any moron could tell you that.

I'd been in love with pop culture my whole life, but now I felt like I was at odds with the entire entertainment universe. Everything was changing. The star system was collapsing. The audience was splintering. The Internet loomed like the Eye of Mordor over the entire media landscape. Not that I could blame my malaise entirely on the ascendance of reality TV and *Transformers* movies, because even the classics had stopped giving me pleasure. One night while I was surfing channels, I happened upon the Marx Brothers' *A Night at the Opera* playing on cable. It should have been a poignant Woody Allen moment, the epiphany when I realized how much joy pop culture had given the whole wide world, how many millions of tears it had dried. Instead, all I could think about was the fact that virtually every single person who appeared in that 1935 film was now dead. Probably even the little kids dancing on the ship deck during the big "Cosi Cosa" number.

I guess you could say I was depressed.

Robin did her best to cheer me up. She set me up with the actress who replaced Purity Love on *DINKs*. Yes, Purity got fired, but not because of her outburst after my article came out. A few months later she made the mistake of sleeping with another new writer on the show. Which would have been fine except he was also the boyfriend of one of the producers. The actress replacing Purity was just as pretty, and no doubt less psychotic, but our date went poorly anyway. My heart just wasn't in it. By the end of the night, we were both in bad moods. "Would you stop that, please," she said, nodding at my hand. I'd been absentmindedly drumming the table with my spoon through most of the meal. How not to pick up chicks.

I tried calling Eliska again. This time I wasn't high and I didn't screw up the time zones. But all I got was her outgoing message. "*Dobry den,*" I heard her recorded voice say. "*Donolali jste sk k Eliska.*" Czech isn't a particularly melodious tongue—it's one hard consonant away from being Klingon—but Eliska made the language sound as soft as a purr. When her message ended, I hung up without saying anything. Then I called back to listen some more. I did this three times before Eliska herself picked up the phone. She'd obviously been screening her calls. "*Prosim?*" she said a little urgently. Flustered, I quickly hung up again.

Even if we had talked, I'm not sure what I would have said. I knew I'd have to explain what had happened, why I had dropped the ball with our e-mail courtship. But that would have meant talking about Samantha, and the last person on Earth I wanted to do that with was Eliska. Sammy's death was emotionally confusing enough; I didn't need to mix those feelings up with the ones I had for my erstwhile would-be Czech mate. What was the point, anyway? Eliska lived a world away. She might as well have been from another galaxy. There was no way it could ever work between us.

In the summer of 2008, I drove my Speedster down to San Diego to attend Comic-Con, the annual geekfest that was beginning to overtake Sundance as the movie industry's most important off-site event. The assignment should have been a blast, like having an all-access pass at nerd Woodstock. For four days every July, more than one hundred thousand fanboys and fangirls from all over the world, many wearing superhero costumes, flocked to the downtown convention center to attend panels with their favorite sci-fi stars, go to screenings of upcoming adaptations of obscure superviolent graphic novels, and purchase pewter miniatures of the USS *Enterprise*. Strolling through the convention floor, I spotted a Hobbit making out with a Sleestak, an Imperial Stormtrooper chatting on a cell phone, and a middle-aged bald guy squeezed into a Superman suit that was two sizes too small. What wasn't to love?

Except I had the worst costume in San Diego. I went as an emotional zombie.

I'd never had less interest in the opposite sex. But in the back of my mind, I thought this trip might rekindle my romance with pop culture, the way bored married couples took a second honeymoon to put some zip back into the relationship. At least if I got that back it would be something recognizable in my life, something comfortable and familiar. So I booked a room at the most expensive place in town, the Hotel del Coronado, just across the bay on Coronado Island. The old Victorian beach resort creaked with age—it had a cage elevator in the lobby that was hand-operated by an attendant in a red jacket who looked like he'd been on duty since the hotel opened in 1888—but it was steeped in movie lore. This was where Jack Lemmon and Tony Curtis dressed up like flappers and shot *Some Like It Hot* in the 1950s. This was where Peter O'Toole blew up one of the hotel's red turrets while shooting *The Stunt Man* in the late 1970s. Not only was I surrounding myself with tens of thousands of hard-core pop culture enthusiasts, but I'd be staying at a genuine cinematic landmark. If this didn't respark the love affair, nothing would.

That first afternoon at Comic-Con, I attended a panel with James Cameron, who screened footage of his upcoming $400 million 3-D remake of *March of the Wooden*

Soldiers. I heard J. J. Abrams talk about his upcoming big-screen adaptation of *Space: 1999,* and Jon Favreau talk about his upcoming live-action version of *The Jetsons*. It all left me cold. Maybe tomorrow would be better. There was an advance screening of *Less Talk, More Killing,* which would be opening nationwide at the end of the summer. I was a little surprised to see the film previewing at Comic-Con. Strictly speaking, Montana movies weren't part of the sci-fi and fantasy genre in that they didn't have aliens or vampires in them. But action films had been making inroads at the convention. They targeted the same demographic: teenage boys of all ages and genders. In any event, I was looking forward to seeing my old friend Jack Montana on the screen again, even if he was now being played by a gay stoner with a pompadour. If anyone could snap me out of my funk, it was my special special agent.

The Hotel del Coronado was supposedly haunted. In 1892, a broken-hearted beauty named Kate Morgan committed suicide in room 305; some say she's been flickering lights and levitating objects at the hotel ever since. I still didn't believe in spirits, but that first night there were some seriously weird noises going on in my room. Low moaning sounds and high-pitched cackling. It could have been the couple next door—I passed them in the hallway earlier, dressed in his-and-her-Wookie outfits—but whatever it was, it was giving me the creeps. I turned on the TV, only I couldn't get the sound to work. A talking gecko was on the screen trying to tell me something. I assumed it had to do with my car insurance. Finally, I switched the set off, put on some clothes, and headed for the cage elevator to take me downstairs to the bar.

The place was hopping, even at one in the morning. Conventioneers and other tourists were drinking and laughing on the bar's patio overlooking the pool. I ordered a vodka on the rocks with extra olives and found a vacant booth in a dark corner. I took a little sip of my drink. Then a bigger one. And then I heard a sound coming from the booth next to mine that was even more startling than the ones in my room—the inimitable stoner baritone of Chuck Fuse. I peeked over into the neighboring booth. For a second, I wondered if it might be a conventioneer in a Chuck Fuse mask. Why else would he be wearing Ray-Ban sunglasses in the middle of the night? But no. It was Fuse.

"Dude!" he said when he saw my head poking over. "Fancy meeting you here. Last time I saw you was in the Bahamas, macking on my assistant." His booming laugh was loud enough to deflate soufflés across a twenty-mile radius. Sitting next to Fuse was an extremely attractive blond woman in her late twenties. There were a Black-Berry and a datebook on the table in front of her. "Dude, sit down." Fuse waved me over. "Meet my assistant, Hillary. She's the new Eliska. How freakin' awesome is this?" He laughed some more. Judging from how friendly he was being, I gathered he liked the story I wrote about him after our interview in the Bahamas. He had every reason to; it was a puff masterpiece. Eliska had inspired me.

"Chuck, what are you doing here?" I asked.

"I'm going to introduce *Less Talk, More Killing* in Hall H tomorrow," he explained. "It's gonna be crazy. The crowd is gonna go nuts."

"It's not on the schedule," I said. "I didn't see anything about you being at Comic-Con in any of the press materials."

"It's a surprise, dude, guerrilla marketing. The studio thought it would be a good idea to get some word of mouth going. Hillary, do you have those screening passes? Let's give a couple to Max, okay?"

"They're in my room," Hillary answered in a boring American accent. "I'll go up and get them. Be right back." She was cute, for sure. Even beautiful. But she wasn't in her predecessor's league.

"So did you and Eliska hook up after the Bahamas?" Fuse asked, as if reading my mind. "She liked you. She was bummed when you left the island. I could tell."

"She mentioned me to you?"

"Well, it's not like we stayed up all night braiding each other's hair while we talked about you, but yeah, she mentioned you. She said she didn't meet guys like you in Prague. You should have gone for it, dude. She was into you."

"It would have been pointless," I said. "We live seven thousand miles apart."

"That's bullshit," Fuse said. "Seven thousand miles is nothing. Miles are just a state of mind. They don't matter. It's a day in an airplane. If you left now, you could be there by"—he looked at his big chunky wristwatch—"four o'clock in the afternoon."

"Actually, it'd be ten o'clock in the morning. I made that mistake once before . . ."

"Whatever, dude," Fuse went on. "Sometimes you gotta say 'What the fuck' and make your move. 'What the fuck' gives you freedom. Freedom brings opportunity. Opportunity makes your future. You know what I mean?"

I knew exactly what he meant. I'd seen *Risky Business,* too.

Hall H was the biggest at the convention center. It sat 6,500 people and had three jumbo screens so that even those in the back rows could see a projection of Fuse's giant head as he strolled onto the stage to introduce *Less Talk, More Killing.* Just as Fuse predicted, the crowd went nuts. Although, from where I was sitting, the crowd looked borderline crazy already. The girl in the seat next to me was wearing Princess Leia's metal bikini from *The Empire Strikes Back.*

The film opened with the Lamborghini chase I had watched being shot in the Bahamas. I was surprised to see that the Lamborghini was neither yellow nor red but green. I wondered how many millions of dollars Gary 7even had set back the production with that color change. But then Jack Montana's jazzy theme music began blasting on the soundtrack and something strange happened to me. The minute I heard those first zippy chords, so familiar from my childhood, I found myself having an out-of-body experience. Or maybe it was out of time. All I know is that while everybody else in Hall H was watching a green Lamborghini chase Fuse around Nassau, I was seeing a different Jack Montana in a different movie.

Johnny Mars was up on the screen, at the peak of his physical powers. He was dodging bullets and blowing away bad guys with a casual coolness that made my heart soar. Sitting next to me in the theater was sixteen-year-old Sammy, so fresh and beautiful I could barely keep my eyes on the film. As Mars climbed the Statue of Liberty, pursued by terrorists in mini-choppers, Sammy took my hand and gave it a warm squeeze. She leaned in and kissed my cheek. I was happy. I was unafraid. The future was still my friend . . .

"Are you okay, mister?" the girl in Princess Leia's bikini asked me. "Are you feeling all right?"

I nodded my head yes but I wasn't all right. I had started to cry. Actually, I had started to sob.

I'd lost everything I cared about. Everything that had made me the person I was, was gone. My love affair with pop culture and movie stars. My decade-long quest to understand fame. Sammy.

I had to get out of there. But except for the light on the screen, Hall H was pitch-black. Tiptoeing out of my row, I tripped over the leg of a guy in a Mighty Morphin Power Ranger costume ("Asshole," he mumbled), landed in the aisle on all fours, got up, and groped my way toward the exit. I finally pushed through the double doors into the blindingly bright corridor outside Hall H. It was packed with conventioneers. A vast, teeming mob of extraterrestrials and supermutants. I tried to elbow my way toward the street exit, but I got pinned between a girl in a Wonder Woman outfit and a guy in Spock ears. I lurched my way free but toppled onto a teenager in a Hulk costume ("Hey, watch where you're going, dickhead," he muttered) as I squirmed through the throng, struggling to get away.

I had made so many mistakes. I had spent my entire adult life with my face pressed up against the windows of other people's lives. I'd interviewed the famous, traveled to the most glamorous locales on Earth, but I'd never been more than an emotional tourist. Even the woman I had loved for all those years—I'd loved her only from afar, from behind the glass wall of her fame. I had devoted myself to a shadow of a girl, a figment, a memory.

I kept pushing through the hordes, my head spinning with regrets. Now that my life had collapsed, I began to see just how wobbly the construction had been all along. I'd built it out of the flimsiest materials—celebrity worship, frequent flyer miles, idealized notions of romantic love. No wonder the thing came crashing down. It was amazing I'd been able to keep it standing for as long as I had. Now I had to build a new life. But how? After being me, who else could I become? Where else could I go? What else could I do?

I finally spotted the plate-glass doors leading to the outside world. I hurled myself toward them with all my might, but it turned out they weren't the exit. They were plate-glass windows. I banged against them headfirst and bounced backward onto the floor. When I got my wind back, I saw three aliens hovering above me. One was a scantily clad reptile woman with four breasts, another looked like a Rastafarian orangutan, and the third—I couldn't believe it—had a furry face and large rodent ears. A conventioneer was made up like my hamsteroid character from *Dark Matter*. What kind of lame fans dressed up like the *extras* from an old sci-fi show?

"Whoa, bro!" hamster man said, looking down at me. "If you want to get out, why don't you just use the door?" I did want to get out—out of everything I'd boxed myself into.

20

The stock market crash wreaked havoc across the entire entertainment-media world in the fall of 2008. Magazines and newspapers were folding right and left. Mass layoffs were spreading across every title at Time Inc., Condé Nast, and Hearst, and firings were rumored to be imminent at *KNOW*, as well. Still, in the midst of the worst financial meltdown since the Great Depression, I found an excuse to jet off to Prague on the company's dime.

The funny thing was, before the economic collapse, I'd been thinking about quitting *KNOW*. In fact, mentally writing my resignation letter had become one of my favorite leisure time activities. The financial apocalypse made me reconsider—it wasn't the smartest time to be pulling out of the labor force—but I was finding it harder and harder to do my job. Every time I sat down with another celebrity and switched on my digital recorder for an interview, a little piece of my soul shriveled up and died. But then, as luck would have it, the Civil War broke out in the one place I'd been looking for an excuse to go, the Czech Republic.

Central Europe was still packed with Hollywood productions. Thanks to a weak currency and cheap labor, it was actually less expensive to fly an entire cast to Prague and build a full-scale replica of the plantation that Ulysses S. Grant used as his military headquarters during the Battle of Chattanooga than it was to shoot the scene at the actual, still-standing plantation in Tennessee. Which is how, in *Ulysses S.*, the great Civil War general ended up invading Confederate territory in Bohemia. And how I ended up on a plane crossing the Atlantic to once again interview the great Alistair Lyon.

The only hitch in my plan was that Eliska didn't want to see me. I finally wrote her an e-mail explaining why I had disappeared so abruptly six months earlier. She replied politely but firmly, offering her condolences for the loss of my friend and best wishes to me for the future, but making it clear she didn't want to have anything more to do with me. I must have really hurt her feelings. Maybe not as badly as her aristo ex-boyfriend, but badly enough. Or else she had simply come to her senses. "It's nice that you are coming to Prague again," she wrote, "but there is no point in seeing each other. Our lives are too different. We live too far away. One of us is bound to get wounded, and I don't want it to be me."

She was right, of course. We did live too far away. Our lives were too different. But, as Chuck Fuse had quoted Curtis Armstrong, sometimes you have to say what the fuck. If Eliska truly was my shot at a second chance, the last train out of the war-torn Berlin that was my romantic life, then I had to make a move. I had to go back to Prague. I had no idea how it would turn out, whether anything could actually happen between us. But I knew I had to try.

So I wrote more e-mails pleading with Eliska to change her mind. I apologized for being such an insensitive clod. I promised to do better in the future. I even offered to bring her a denim catsuit with an ABBA patch—"So America!" I wrote—if she'd have just one cup of coffee with me. Eventually, I wore her down and she relented. She agreed to meet me in Old Town Square. But this time, she made clear, there would be no drinking of Becherovka. And definitely no kissing.

As with all his roles, Lyon threw himself into the part of General Grant with an intensity that would have had Robert De Niro and Russell Crowe elbowing each other and rolling their eyes. He spent seven months on the facial hair alone, growing and trimming until he got the beard and mustache precisely right. He read dozens of biographies, pored over tintype photographs taken during the Civil War, even consulted historians on what the future eighteenth president's voice sounded like. The consensus, judging from the scratchy, whiskey-soaked snarl Alistair ultimately settled on, was a combination of the Dark Knight and a broken garbage disposal.

"My friend!" Alistair greeted me when I arrived on the field in the suburbs of Prague where the Battle of Chattanooga was about to be re-created. Alistair was outfitted in a Union officer's dress uniform and carrying an unsheathed sword with a golden pommel. A hundred extras in sack coats and forage caps were sitting on the grass in front of the facade of a fake antebellum manse that had been erected for the scene. Horses with nineteenth-century military saddles were grazing nearby. "We really must stop meeting like this," the star joked. Then he put his arm around my shoulder and walked me toward a couple of rocking chairs on the fake mansion's real-enough porch, where we could conduct the interview until the shooting began.

There was a time when this sort of cozy rapport with a star would have thrilled me. I would have relished the jealous glances I was drawing from the cast and crew. I would have felt special, important, higher up on the food chain, as Suki Monroe put it. But not anymore.

Oh, I liked Alistair well enough. In a way, bumping into him all those times, especially at Sammy's memorial, had made him the closest thing I had to a friend in the celebrity world. But I didn't care about his General Grant movie, about his acting, about any of the things I was supposed to be writing about for KNOW magazine. All I wanted was to get the interview over with so that I could get back to my hotel room in time to change before meeting Eliska at the clock tower in Old Town Square at six that evening, as we had arranged in our last e-mail exchange. That was all this trip to Prague was about.

"How is your philosophical study of fame going?" Alistair asked me as I set up my voice recorder, testing the microphone the way I had a hundred times before. "Have you unlocked the secret yet?"

"I gave up caring," I answered honestly. "The whole thing started to seem silly. I don't think there is any big secret. As far as I can tell, people look wherever the camera is pointed. It doesn't matter who it's pointed at. You're famous because it happens to be pointed at you a lot of the time. If it were pointed at me, I'd be famous too."

Alistair tapped his nose with a finger. "Exactly," he said. "Congratulations. You have figured out the secret. Too bad for you."

"Why too bad?" I asked.

"Because now your job is going to be a lot less fun. Now you know the truth. The camera has all the magical powers. The people you interview aren't special at all. They don't have any magic. They just happen to be in front of cameras. How boring."

"I guess I'll have to find something else to write about," I said, turning on the voice recorder.

The traffic on the highway into Prague made me want to take back all the rotten things I'd ever said about the 405 freeway. It took the production crew's transport van more than an hour to travel the twenty kilometers to my hotel near Wenceslas Square. I barely had time to change my shirt before meeting Eliska. I was halfway out the door when the phone on the desk began chirping in its exotic European way. I made the mistake of picking it up.

"Max, you better get on the next flight to New York," Carla said. She sounded even more stressed than usual. "There's a bloodbath going on over here."

"What are you talking about, Carla?" I really didn't have time for this. It was already five-thirty.

"Layoffs, Max. They're laying off a quarter of the staff. The stock market dropped another six hundred points today. It's sheer bedlam. You should get back here."

I stood frozen with the phone to my ear. I couldn't speak. It was happening—I was finally getting out, and I didn't even have to write a resignation letter. I was being fired. My pulse was racing. It was petrifying but also, I couldn't deny it, thrilling.

"It's terrible, Max," Carla went on. "I'm so upset I smashed my Al Gore snow globe against the wall. At least they're giving people decent severances. One month's salary for every year you've worked here. That should help take some of the sting out of it, but still . . ."

I did some quick math. I'd been at the magazine fourteen years. I'd be getting over a year's salary! The possibilities were breathtaking. Together with the miles in my frequent flyer account, I could go anywhere in the world and do anything I wanted, at least for a while. Total, absolute freedom—how often does that opportunity get dangled in front of you? Or else, I thought, maybe I'd just stick around Prague for a while. That sounded pretty appealing, too.

"Well," I finally said, "I'm really going to miss you, Carla. You've always been good to me. Don't think I don't appreciate it . . ."

"What? No, wait a second, Max," she interrupted. "You're not getting laid off, you moron. You're getting promoted. You're the new bureau chief. That's why you should get back here. There's a big meeting at the end of the week. You should show your face at it. It'd be a smart political move for you."

"This can't be right," I said, stunned. "What about D. B. Martin? He's the bureau chief! He's always been the bureau chief."

"Fired," Carla said. "At least he will be if we can ever find him. You don't know where he is, by any chance?"

I was devastated. In the course of a five-minute phone conversation, I'd tasted the sweet air of liberty, only to be shoved back into my cage, the door clanging shut on my nose. I didn't want to be bureau chief! Yes, okay, at one point I'd have killed for the job. Hanging out with celebrities day and night, being accepted by them as if I were one of their own, having them suck up to *me* for a change— there was a time when I would have found all that beyond irresistible. Now, though, the idea made my stomach turn. There was no way I could do it. I held the phone to my chest for a second. I was having trouble breathing.

"Carla," I said, the words coming out of my mouth almost before I realized I was saying them, "fire me. Lay me off. I'm begging you."

I made it to the clock tower at six on the button. I know because Death started gonging his bell the second I arrived. There was still some daylight left in the slate-gray sky, and the cobblestone square was full of tourists taking pictures and feeding crumbs to the pigeons. I planted myself conspicuously in front of the clock tower and waited for Eliska. And waited. And waited some more.

After fifteen minutes, I sat down on a bench and began to lick my wounds. She wasn't coming. I'd made the trip to Prague for nothing. I watched as people ambled past me in the square. A sweet old couple holding each other's arms. A family with a baby in a stroller. Two skinheads kicking a soccer ball. I began to wonder if quitting my job had been such a brilliant decision. All I wanted to do now was curl up on my sofa in Venice with a remote control and a bag of cheese puffs. I sighed, buttoned up my coat, and was about to get to my feet.

"You thought I upstood you again?" Eliska said. She was suddenly in front of me, out of breath. "I'm sorry I'm late, but they stopped tram service at Vozovna Vokovice again. I had to run the whole way here. I don't know why they keep shutting down that station . . ."

I was so relieved I jumped up and almost gave Eliska a kiss. I stopped myself just in time. Her cheeks were flushed and her honey-blond hair was a tangled mess from her rush from school to the square, but she was even lovelier than I remembered. I couldn't stop staring into her big green eyes. She stared back with a curious gaze. "Are you okay?" she asked. "You look like you've heard a ghost."

"*Seen* a ghost," I corrected her. "And I'm fine, really. I'm great. It's just so wonderful to see you again. I was afraid you weren't coming."

"No," she said, studying my face. "You are not fine. I can see that very clearly. You've been through a lot. You look different somehow."

"Different in a good way or a bad way?" I asked.

"I don't know yet," she said. "I'll let you know when I decide." Then she smiled, took my hand in hers, and walked with me across the old cobblestone square.

21

The big block letters on the marquee spell out the words JOHNNY MARS IN "LIVE FREE OR KILL." Next to the ticket office, inside a poster display case, is a one-sheet with an illustration of Jack Montana dangling from the Statue of Liberty's torch. Outside the theater it's beginning to snow. Sammy and I are standing on the sidewalk, zipping up our coats, about to start the walk back home. We are sixteen years old.

"I get to choose the next movie," Samantha says. "And I'm telling you now—it's going to have subtitles."

"Oh, c'mon," I say. "Are you telling me you didn't like this movie? That scene in the power plant with the killer Nazi gymnast? When Jack Montana drops her down the ventilation shaft and says, 'Just letting off some steam.' You didn't love that?"

"It was okay," Sammy says. "But you know I'm not as big a fan of Johnny Mars as you are. I honestly don't understand what you see in the guy."

"He's cool," I try to explain. "He can handle any situ-

ation. No matter what happens, he's always in control. I'd give anything to be like that."

"You don't have to be an action hero," Sam tells me. "I like you just the way you are."

I grab her by the waist and lift her up, the way Jack Montana did with the Nazi gymnast in the power plant. "Just letting off some steam," I joke as I carry her down the snowy sidewalk. She laughs and kicks until I put her down and let her go.